Between Two Wars

Robert S. Telford

Order this book online at www.trafford.com
or email orders@trafford.com

Most Trafford titles are also available at major online book retailers.

Printed in the United States of America.

ISBN: 978-1-4669-2965-4 (sc)
ISBN: 978-1-4669-2966-1 (hc)
ISBN: 978-1-4669-2964-7 (e)

Library of Congress Control Number: 2012906738

Trafford rev. 04/12/2012

North America & international
toll-free: 1 888 232 4444 (USA & Canada)
phone: 250 383 6864 • fax: 812 355 4082

Chapter One

Two steps at a time up the stoop of the brownstone on West 105th Street. Howie twisted the great brass knob, all but riding the door into the lobby and froze, listening, listening for the raucous voice of his Aunt Nana and the sweet, sweet sound of the girl he'd brought down from Springfield, the girl he was going to marry—Ellie—Eleanor Arlington. He closed the front door quietly, intending to surprise them, perhaps spy on them, feeling sure that he would hear from the parlor down the hall only passion from his bride-to-be and praise from Nana.

"Dear, do you really know what kind of a man he is, do you really know that much about him?"

Nana's voice stopped his breathing like a switch. *What was Nana doing? What did she mean by " . . . what kind of man he is"?*

"I know he's sweet, and he's kind, thoughtful . . . "

Nana cut her off. "And he's morose and cranky. He has inward grouches that are like mental indigestion . . . "

"Oh, he's not that." Ellie was laughing now.

"My dear, Howard is very intelligent, very talented, and I know he's going to be very successful. You'll not want for a place to lay your head. But he can be very difficult. You can't hide that. He can't. And you need to know that as you enter into marriage with him."

There was a long pause before and after an unexpected request.

"Tell me about his mother."

He could hear Nana pull in her breath, imagine her yanking at her corset.

"My baby sister was a beautiful girl. Not like me," she added, laughing. "But she was very much her own person. There were eight of us children, and—next to the youngest—Laura Augusta took life as though it had been handed to her on a silver platter. She expected it so, and she never felt she owed anything in return."

"Howard says very little of her."

"That's because I think he got very little from her."

Howie heard one of Nana's little snorts, the kind that came with her critical eye, the kind that said her own behavior was better. "You have to remember that she's been gone over a decade, now. Howard may not miss her, may not even remember her, but he's got the blood of Augusta Hampson in him. Before you came to visit, his room was a pig-pen, clothes lying on the floor just where he took them off. He's just as much a flibberty-gibbet as his mother."

"And his father?"

"George is a dear. He has a wonderful laugh, he works hard, he loves people, and he can be a clever devil. But he has about as much chance of a success in this country as he had back in Scotland."

"Howard's not like that." He could almost hear Ellie's breathing.

Nana sighed. "No, he'll probably do all right. I don't like to say this, but I don't think he's ever forgiven his mother for dying or his father for letting her do it."

"What did she die of?"

"The dropsy. There was a bad spell of it here, and she swelled up like a porcupine. It was sad. She went fast. They were living over on

66th Street then, and the Baptist Church across from them arranged for Howard to go to C.L.I., that Academy in Suffield where he met you. His sister, Laura, went with one of my other sisters. For a while. She was not very happy there. I wasn't surprised."

"Howard almost never talks about his father. He calls my parents 'Ma' and 'Pa.' Even 'Dad,' sometimes. Where does Howard's father live?"

"In Philadelphia. He travels. Selling books."

Howard could imagine her cocking her head, eyebrows heading for the ceiling as she said it. He started back toward the front door. Before he turned away he heard:

"Howard loves me. He's loved me all through school. He doesn't know that I know that, but I do. And he knows that I haven't always been nice to him, but he has been patient, steadfast, and always kind to me. I will be good to him," she went on hesitantly, "and I know that the pain of losing his mother—his whole family—will be something we'll have to live with. But, Nana, we will have each other, and whatever sadness there has been I will help erase it. That is why God has brought us together. That is why Howard . . . . "

He didn't wait for any more. He was out of earshot before she'd finished, wrenching the door handle and calling out, "I'm home!"

He slammed the door shut, making sure the noise carried all the way to the parlor, and once again he started down the hall.

Chapter Two

Howard stared at the envelope in his right hand. It had arrived on his desk the Friday before, fresh with the morning's mail. The West Springfield, Mass. post mark and the date October 2, 1916 covered the two-cent stamp. A tiny, scrunched "M. Arlington" with return address crowded into the up left corner. However, it was addressed to him not at his apartment up on West 105th Street with Aunt Nana and Uncle Apsley but at the New York Sun and in a large, flamboyant, almost balletic scrawl. He'd never seen the penmanship before, but the two different styles matched the dual personality, the withdrawn and the florid, of Ellie's baby sister Maude. It surprised him that Maude had written to him at all, but the contents had been even more startling.

The letter began simply and directly, to the point: "Elmore has gone to New Mexico." And that was really all he needed to know. The rest went on to describe—or try to describe—Ellie's reaction to the departure of the person Howard and all the Suffield gang had imagined was Ellie's intended. What puzzled him was what Maude referred to as Ellie's total lack of response.

Howard had to work that weekend, but today was Monday, His day off, and he was firmly on board the New York, New Haven and Hartford railroad. The train pulled out of Grand Central Station, and Howard stared at the cement walls, the train's reflected sight and sound bombarding his already addled brain.

Eighty blocks of underground between Grand Central and the 125th Street Station magnified his sense of claustrophobia. Overhead was Park Avenue, free, breezy, ritzy East Side New York. But to the west, covering the same stretch of crosstown streets, was "Hell's Kitchen," the rough and tumble vault where he had grown up. East and west of Central Park were worlds apart.

Lights flashing on the cement walls dropped away when the Park Avenue tunnel widened out and slammed back when the walls moved to within inches. He could see his face in the glass between, drawn, almost haggard for a man only twenty-three years old.

The paramount thing about those "Hell's Kitchen" days was the number of times the family had moved. First it was on 51st Street, over near the river. Then it was on Ninth Avenue a few blocks up. There'd been dozens more. Every time the rooms got dirty they'd up and move because Augusta Andrews loathed housecleaning. At least that was the way Howard remembered his mother. Every neighborhood was a new gang of kids. He hated trying to assimilate, getting to know the other guys, to be known, to be liked. He hated that. And he despised baby-sister Laura's gift for popping into a new area and making friends as quickly as they came her way.

Books were Howard's world. And, although he despised giving him credit for a single thing, it was his father he had to thank, a book salesman who traveled through upstate New York and west across Pennsylvania and back down again to New York City. The Andrews household was always full of the classics, Yeats, Stevenson, Virgil, Homer, *The Iliad, The Odyssey.* And O. Henry. And Poe!

Howard loved O. Henry and the surprises, the ironies such as in "The Gift of the Magi." But he liked the wonderful darkness in

Poe and especially the contrasting and beautiful poem of "Annabel Lee." Howard's dream was of "Annabel Lee." An "Annabel Lee" of his own. He saw her with beautiful blonde hair, willowy and gentle, considerate, giving.

The Andrews family ended up right across the street from the Baptist Church on West Sixty-Sixth Street where his mother went every Sunday. And while she attended services, his father slept or walked over to Central Park and around the lakes. He said it was because there was no Presbyterian Church in the neighborhood. After all, he was a Scotsman, and no Baptist was going to preach to him. His thick Scottish burr made him a colorful salesman, but it was accompanied by a sharp, flaring temper.

His father's temper and his mother's messy housekeeping: that's what Howard remembered about "Hell's Kitchen."

It was when they were living on West 66th Street that everything fell apart. His mother caught the "dropsy" and died within weeks. George couldn't leave two children in a Manhattan apartment, so he shuffled Laura off to one of Augusta's sisters and gave Howard to the Baptist Church.

In Suffield, Connecticut, there was a seminary created to "train pious young men to serve as preachers for destitute Baptist churches." When it opened in 1832, it was called the Connecticut Baptist Literary Institution. The word "Baptist" was soon dropped, and it became known as the Connecticut Literary Institution . . . or, affectionately, C.L.I. For the Connecticut Valley children, C.L.I. came to serve as a Suffield area public school, as well as a repository for boys bereft of the normal complement of parents . . . and who, in addition, might be pointed toward piety.

Howard certainly wasn't pious, had no intention of being so and didn't realize he was a Baptist, but he had learned quickly just what an orphan was. And he never forgave his mother for making him one or his father for farming him out as one. Never mind what Laura went through, it was his own misery, his own unwantedness that he carried into that quiet, conservative, moderate, tranquil town.

Bitter and sullen, clutching his volume of Edgar Allan Poe with its smudged pages of "Annabel Lee," Howard walked into "Prof" Cliff Granger's class and slung himself into the last seat next to the windowed wall. It was the fall of 1906. Howard would be fifteen in November. Boys straggled in, laughing, brooding, racing, shuffling, filling the room. Then there were the girls. Half-a-dozen of them! Skinny ones, fat ones, short ones, ugly ones. They were the Suffield kids. He realized that so were some of the boys. But which ones were the orphans? At least they would understand. He would feel less lonely. That bothered him.

Then a tall girl with golden hair in two pigtails tied with black ribbon bows, a tall girl with fathomless blue eyes and an infectious laugh and a lissome figure, an angel not unlike "Annabel Lee," glided gently into the room. She sat in the back of the room, too, but in the opposite corner.

The fall semester of 1906 wore on. Disappointingly, Howard's "Annabel Lee" didn't seem to recognize her Edgar Allan Poe. Gradually word reached him as to why. And his name was Elmore Whittle.

Eleanor Arlington lived right on Suffield's main street. Her father's "tent tobacco" farm stretched from behind the house to far in the north. Elmore's house was cattie-corner across the street, and it was simple and natural that he could cross over each morning and join Ellie and her younger sister, Maude, on the trek down to C.L.I.

It was early in the history of that ritual that Elmore had fallen in behind the two girls and called out, "Ellie, your petti's showing." Under ordinary circumstances that could have proven embarrassing as Eleanore handed her books to Maude and dropped back behind the advancing Elmore to tug at her shoulder straps and haul her petticoat up under the skirt where it belonged. But Elmore was old-shoe to the Arlingtons, the kid who lived across the street, who grew up with them and had no more prominence in their lives but the fact of being.

When she caught up with Maude, the younger sister had handed Ellie's books off to Elmore, and thus began the ritual of Elmore Whittle carrying Eleanor Arlington's books to school. Through the years, C.L.I. considered them a twosome, and as graduation approached, it was natural the he would be looked upon as Ellie's intended. However, despite the fact that she liked Elmore, she simply took him for granted, a boy who could carry her books and be an escort to the school plays.

Howard, on the other hand, had pleaded his case and gained something of a reputation for chasing Ellie. Even after he graduated in 1909 and signed on with the Hartford Courant for a struggling $10-a-week, he used his Sundays to travel the "Huckleberry," a branch line of the New Haven Railroad that linked Hartford to Suffield. There he headed for the Arlington house just up the street from C.L.I., slowing down to a meander at his destination so as not to look too eager.

"Hello, Howie," Maude would say. She knew when he was coming along and waited for him on the side porch. It was devilish, he knew, but he was grateful for the ice-breaker just the same.

"Whatcha' doin' in town, Howie?" she teased.

"Oh, nuthin'. I . . . . " And then his voice would trail off.

"Ellie's not home," Maude would go on, Howie's face going through various gyrations while Maude stifled a giggle. "She's out on the hill sketching the tobacco," she'd say, or "She's down at the soda shop," or maybe even, "She's off with Elmore this morning. They went to church today." When she used that one she cocked her head to one side so she could watch him without seeming to look at him. He got to recognize that look quite well, and he realized more than once that she was making a lot of it up.

Most of the time he was able to track Ellie down. Mostly because she was sketching. She usually did that on Sundays after church.

He'd find her on that hill overlooking Pa's tobacco fields, a huge pad of ocher paper cradled in her lap and half a dozen sticks of charcoal and sharply pointed pencils in her apron pocket.

"Hi, Ellie."

"Why, Howie! What a surprise. What're doing in Suffield this Sunday?"

He never knew whether to take that seriously or not. But serious was safer.

"Oh, I just sort of meandered on over," he'd say.

"All the way from Hartford?" She and Maude had the same sly, head-cocked way of being funny.

"Well, . . . " Finally he'd give in and admit that he'd been teased. But only to himself. He'd sit down with her, look out over the fields and reckon that Heaven had to be a little bit like this.

"Want to do some sketching?"

"No, I'd rather just watch you."

She looked at him quickly, a slight grin below twinkling eyes. It made him feel witty and clever and very much appreciated. That was worth any day back and forth on the "Huckleberry."

At the end of that school year, it was Ellie's turn to graduate. And it was also Elmore's. It was 1910, and all Howie knew was that Ellie was going to Mount Holyoke College for Women. He didn't know about Elmore, and he was too afraid to ask. It turned out that Elmore went to Pre-Med in Boston, the best thing that could have happened.

Ellie moved on up the Connecticut River to Holyoke and to help make up the class of 1914, an accomplishment that certainly outclassed Howard's. His "Annabel Lee" was now even further removed. But she was still his angel—deferred perhaps, more distant perhaps—but ultimately accessible, he firmly believed.

Howard immersed himself in his reporting. His reading shifted from Virgil and Homer to "The Saturday Evening Post" and "Liberty Magazine." The serials there were full of excitement, suspense and irony. Assembly line O. Henry, he called them. He swore he could do as well. During his off hours, he scribbled pages and pages of dramatic irony.

When the Hartford Currant announced that William Sidney Porter, the fabled "O. Henry," was gone, Howard saw himself as the successor to the creator of strange twists, magical paradoxes and fateful destinies. Better still, he'd be the writer and illustrator! He clipped episodes from the "Post" and mailed them to Ellie along with sketches of his own. Better than the ones printed with the serial! So he felt.

But he held back on his own fiction, squirreled it away in his desk. Not yet were his stories ready for her to read. One day they'd be right. And she'd read them. She'd smile that same, head-to-one-side smile, but this time it would be an embracing smile. "Annabel Lee" would respond. Certainly she would. She would have to.

Chapter Three

In the years that followed, a weekend or two wandering around Suffield did him good, even knowing that Ellie was miles away at Mount Holyoke.

"Hi, Howie, whatcha doing here?"

It was Maude's same old line, but the joke had become a nice one they shared. He liked Ellie's younger sister. Not like his own, Laura the brat who laughed and acted silly and ran up and down the sidewalk in Hell's Kitchen. Laura had teased him, but teased him because he was backward or stupid or just because he was so serious half the time. Maude teased him because she knew he was clever. He firmly believed that, too.

"Just wandering around the old town."

"Ellie's up at the house."

He wasn't sure she wasn't kidding. "Really?"

"Honest. Want to come up to the house? Get you a cold drink," she half urged.

But when they stepped into the parlor, the scene was not what he'd expected. And it was apparently not what Maude had anticipated, either.

"What's all this?" Maude said from the doorway. Across the room, Pa was seated by the little tobacco stand talking to Ellie who was riveted, bolt upright, smack in the middle of the horsehair sofa. Ma was on this side of the room, just to the left of the doorway. She was the one who spoke.

"Come in and sit down, Maude." It was then her eyes met Howie's. Her chin went up slightly, and she took a quick breath, but her eyes never altered from the cool, crystalline gaze she bestowed on everyone, family and strangers alike. It never wavered, even as Howard's eyes bounced around the room from one unresponsive face to another. When he looked back at her, she was already speaking.

"Howard, I wonder if you wouldn't mind waiting out on the porch. I'm sure the girls will be through in a little while, and then you can visit."

Howard nodded, wordlessly, and backed out almost to the porch itself. He straddled one of the canvass, sling back chairs and stared at his fingernails for what seemed like an eternity.

"I'm sorry, Howie. I hope we weren't rude." Ellie came through the screen door, and Howard leaped to his feet, tangling himself in the footrest. There was a moment's awkwardness. He knew something terrible had happened.

"I'm leaving Holyoke," Ellie began. *Why,* his head screamed. And then, *great!*, it answered. *She'll be here where we can see each other.* The logic begged for a voice, but he was too frozen to do more than mumble something even he couldn't decipher.

But then Ellie dropped the bombshell.

"Pa's lost the farm."

The words crashed down. This was the last thing he'd expected. How could that wonderful man . . . .

"The bank's taking it over. He's not even going to be able to harvest this year's crop of leaf tobacco. The bank's going to do it.

I suppose you might as well know it all, since everyone will know eventually. Soon," she added. "I'm finishing the year at Holyoke and then coming home at the end of the Spring semester." She moved over to the railing and put her hand on the post.

It was a sketch, he thought, *almost Greek-like, begging to be immortalized on canvass.* Immediately he lacerated himself for his insanity at such a time of catastrophe. *Help her, help her,* his mind cried. Silence.

Ellie turned to him, calm and with a sweetness that was as reasonable as it was unreasonable. "I'll get a job teaching in Springfield, and . . . . " She stopped a moment. "I forgot to mention. We're moving to Springfield, across the state line. Pa can get a job there. I'm sure I can get one teaching. I'll be a sophomore at Holyoke when I leave, so there shouldn't be any problem getting a teaching job."

The screen door behind her banged against the house as Maude planted herself in the opening. "Yes, you'll have two years at Holyoke, but what will I have? I was going to Framingham, but now I won't have a thing, will I?," she snapped.

Eleanor didn't turn her head. Her eyes played along the porch deck as she answered gently, "Maude, that won't stop you from making something of your life." Then she turned. "And you will have me. I will help you. I promise."

Howard's heart was bursting. *Oh, God, give me the wits to talk, to say something at least a little like that!* But there was no room. Maude stepped to Eleanor for a brief moment.

"Ma is right. Pa's a drunk, and he's a fool, and he's dragged this whole family down while he's destroyed himself." She swung around the post and down the steps, on out around the barn and off into the tobacco fields that were no longer Arlington fields.

When the sun had gone down, Ellie and Howard wandered around the C.L.I. campus and came to rest on the steps of Memorial Building where they had shared classes. All Howard wanted to do was to comfort her, but his mind kept grinding and conniving and plotting. *Profit from the situation, scoop up the damsel in distress, take command*, he told himself. *No. That's not taking command, that's taking advantage*, his conscience argued.

Ellie had all but talked herself out, and so they sat on the cold stone in silence. Before he could think it through, he heard himself saying:

"Ellie, I know I don't have any money, a big paying job, but I know I can be a big success, and I think you like me—a little—and I know I'll have a lot of money some day, and even though your father probably won't let you, will you wait for me?"

It was the old "You don't know nobody don't want no work done, do you?" syndrome. And it worked just about as well. She simply smiled, leaned her head against his shoulder for a moment and then looked far off across the lawn and down the road. Finally she sighed, "Oh, Howard, you're so sweet. I'm really sorry."

In the years that followed, the Arlington family settled into a long, rangy house in West Springfield along the banks of the beautiful Connecticut River. Maude built a chicken coup and began peddling eggs while she looked for a regular job. Ellie got a position teaching in a one-room school house. Elmore graduated from college and stayed in Boston to complete medical school.

Howard intensified his trips over on the Huckleberry, and Ellie had to ask him to stop.

"Not *every weekend*, Howie! And no more letters and postcards either."

"You don't like my post cards?" He tried to get her to smile.

"Howie, when you draw my picture on the back of a postcard as the girl in your pipe dreams, everyone in the house—in the post office, even—knows what you're saying."

He was ready to gamble that even Elmore knew about the sketches. They'd probably driven Ellie and Elmore even closer together than they'd been back at C.L.I. when Elmore had lived just across the street. Howard was losing her, and it was more than he could cope with believing that his insistence was directly to blame.

Fate and Howard's talents stepped in at the right time. After three years on the Courant, he was invited to join the staff of the prestigious New York Sun as a night reporter with the respectable salary of $25-a-week!

Manhattan was miles from Springfield, but it wasn't too far for surprise visits. On many a Monday-off, Howard took the New York, New Haven and Hartford to Springfield and popped in on Ellie's little schoolhouse to nurture his devotion.

They sat beneath their favorite schoolyard tree and talked about his dreams, newspaper reporter to short story writer to world famous novelist. They read to each other, serial stories in "The Saturday Evening Post," "Liberty Magazine," "The Ladies Home Journal." But each evening when they harnessed Nellie to the buggy and Ellie drove him over to the Springfield station, Howard felt no closer to his aspiration for her than he had been the night before, nodding off in his Aunt Nana's apartment up on Manhattan's West 105th Street.

Four more years passed. Ellie taught in her one-room school house, Howard struggled unsuccessfully to move from night reporter to one with a regular downtown beat. Everything would have seemed mired in unyielding slough were it not for an obscure man named Princip. Shortly before noon on Sunday, July 28, 1914, Princip jumped on the automobile running board of Archduke Francis Ferdinand, heir to the throne of Austria-Hungary, and fired a pistol. Gavrilo Princip, a young Bosnian student from Serbia had, in essence, started World War One.

President Wilson promised not to go to war, but the country was warming up, and Howard saw himself standing ready to defend his flag.

Howard kept Maude's letter in his hand, removing it from the crumpled envelope, unfolding it carefully and reading it over and over for signs of suggestion, hints of direction. The train made its usual stop at Manhattan's 125th Street and then began the long haul through New Haven and Hartford on to Springfield, Massachusetts.

As the ride lengthened, Howard turned to the pile of manuscripts he'd bundled up to bring along. Lying on the seat beside him, they looked less like the accomplishments he'd intended to boast and more like foolish undertakings, scraps of failure. But they were his best columns—byline deficient, unfortunately—along with little essays about New York, the newspaper business and life with the upper crust, most of which he knew little about. And then there were his first drafts of fiction, the sketches of romance and daring-do, ripe for magazine serials, stories that, with a little of Ellie's help, might rival the late O. Henry.

The yanking, snapping, bouncing vibration of the train shook the sheets like residue from a trash barrel. Slipping, sliding about the mohair upholstery, they offered little to bolster his security. He wanted to push the pile onto the floor except that he knew he'd only have to clean it up.

It was a long walk from the end of the West Springfield trolley line to Ellie's little schoolhouse, a walk that never failed to buoy him and peek his fragile hopes. What would she think of his manuscripts? What about his newspaper stories? Ah, hah! What about his new moustache? It disguised his nether lip. Fellow reporters thought it made him look more mature, and, after all, that was why he grew it.

The schoolhouse doorway was open. Fall leaves garlanded the pathway from the lane to the sound of laughter, a ruler's persistent tap and admonitions for attention. Howard approached from the off side, where the students couldn't see him but Ellie would.

"Stop! Stop! Stop! Henry! Leave her alone!" Tap, tap. "Henry, you're going to have to stay late!"

She finally caught his eye. Her sudden silence and softened smile turned the entire class around, engulfed in the same hush.

Hi, Ellie!, he mouthed.

Her smile emerged full blown just as the class returned to pandemonium. Howard pointed to their favorite tree and waved a goodbye-for-now.

"You like it?"

"I don't know." She grinned sideways at the moustache. "You do look very distinguished. Very handsome," she added almost in a tease.

They shared silence for a moment. Then she spoke.

"I'm going to quit teaching for a while and go to Pratt Institute and learn more . . . "

"In Brooklyn? We'll be right next door!"

There was a touch of smile when she answered: "I know."

Howard spilled everything, his love, his adoration, his new, improved proposal . . . with emphasis on $45-a-week.

"Oh, Howard, do you really care for me . . . still?"

Even in that moment there was one long string of embarrassments. He had trouble finding her lips. But the crash of uncertain years all falling away was almost deafening.

Elmore's name wasn't mentioned. And they never got around to reading Howard's short stories.

Chapter Four

"Whatya' mean you're getting married? You're not even going with anybody."

"It's a girl I went with at Suffield Academy."

"Oh, my Gawd, it's 'Annabel Lee'!"

Howard shifted his rifle to bayonet-thrust and growled, "Tommy, behave yourself or I won't let you be Best Man."

Tommy Ross howled: "Best Man! Yeow! You're pickin' me for Best Man?"

Howard and Tommy were two of the "bright young men" on the New York Sun. Together they had monitored the world situation and determined that, despite Wilson's promise to "keep our boys from going to war," they absolutely knew we'd be in it before long. In the spring of 1915 they and a handful of other reporters from Manhattan, the Bronx, Brooklyn and Long Island formed the Cadet Newspaper Men's Training Corps.

Crowded onto a spot of land in the New York harbor called Governors Island, Ft. Jay held a small but potent garrison where Major Harrison Hall taught rookies to do close order drill and disassemble a Springfield and an Eddystone Enfield. "Harrison's Garrison," they called it—behind his back. The Major was proud of his men and so impressed with some of them that he wrote letters recommending commissions if they were ever called up. Howard was one, and he was ecstatic!

Howard and Ellie had set the date for August 17, 1917 and received permission from the elder Arlingtons. Pa gave the expected handclasp and pat on the shoulder, but it was Ma's reaction Howard most feared. She looked him right in the eye, all right, but it wasn't till she took in Ellie's smile that she nodded and said, "I approve." Maude, of course, just snorted and grinned, but Howard knew she had no complaints.

Maude had had it rough when they first moved to West Springfield. Just out of C.L.I., she was a newcomer in a neighborhood where she knew nobody. The chickens she raised proved a good ice breaker, though, and soon she was peddling eggs and fryers throughout the neighborhood. But that wasn't enough, so when she heard of an opening on the staff of the Springfield Girls Club, she leaped at the chance.

"I think you should have the wedding right here on the lawn," Maude broke in. "I can get some of the girls to come over and put up lanterns. We'll have the ceremony at night. And we can decorate the lawn right down to the river."

"And the chickens can sing 'Here Comes the Bride'," added Ma.

"Oh, they'll keep quiet. Heck, I'll chop off all their heads if they won't keep still."

"Watch your language, young lady," Ma admonished.

Pa was looking out the window behind his tobacco stand. "You know, that'd calculate to make a real nice ceremony. Out there underneath that apple tree. The rose arbor all lit up with candles and lanterns and such. I kinda' like that."

Ma was watching Ellie closely. She seemed to warm to what she saw because she went to her, took her hand and patted it. "You come on into the dining room and set a spell while I fix us some tea."

Back in New York, Howard wrote a letter to his father and sister Laura in Philadelphia. The wedding was still almost a year off, but he owed them some warning at least. Then he came down from his room to the parlor on the Bouldings' 105th Street brownstone and broke the news to his Aunt Nana and her husband Apsley.

"Howard, you know we'd love you to stay on here with your bride, but that's the only room we've got, and you know it's kinda' small."

"Not that you're not welcome," added Apsley.

"Nana, we're not going to live here!" Howard had to control his irritation over this stodgy old lady's inability to keep up with his goings on. "I'm getting an apartment downtown, nearer the Sun, and we'll make a home there."

"On twenty-five dollars a week?" she whined.

"Oh, Nan, for Gawd's sake," bawled Apsley, "give the boy a break. He knows what he's doing, and the two of them will make out just fine. When are we going to meet her," he added.

Howard hadn't thought of that. "I'll bring her in some weekend this fall," he answered quickly. He considered taking her to meet Laura and his father in Philadelphia, but that was too much to tackle at this time. Besides, he wasn't sure he wanted to show them that much concern.

By the spring of 1917, the world had turned inside out. Just three and a half months before the wedding date, on April 6th, President Wilson crimped their plans with a call to arms. Bowing to the President's wishes, Congress declared war on the Kaiser, and on May 3rd Howard, Tommy Ross and several others from the Cadet Newspaper Men's Training Corps were sent to Plattsburg in upstate New York for Infantry Officer's Candidate School. The "90-Day-Wonder" training session made it a close cut for an August 17th wedding.

Three months of lectures, quizzes, foot-paced map making, military courtesy training, squad, platoon, company and battalion drill from reveille at 5:30 in the morning to taps at 9:30 P.M. culminated in a close-order march into the Camp Auditorium for the final ceremony. Howard, Tommy and their new friends looked around to see who was missing, who had "washed out." They were still recounting names when their's were called.

"Lieutenant Howard G. Andrews."

A step forward, a sharp salute and a hand outstretched for the steel engraved parchment attested to his appointment as Second Lieutenant, Infantry, by the President of the United States. Outside, the spanking new "shavetails" lined up to receive their first salute and bestow the traditional crisp new dollar bills on their favorite enlisted men.

That night, Howard snipped the tail off his khaki shirt to cut, fold and stitch onto the shoulders of his shirt the epaulets that distinguished him as a "shavetail." Then he soaked his gold bars in a glass of salt water so they wouldn't look brand new.

"Howey, I've put in for Artillery School."

Howard stared at Tommy. "Whatdya' mean?"

"I mean I'm not for this slogging through the mud, the trenches waiting for us in France, the bayonet in the belly kind of warfare. You see those fellows over in the Fifth Training Area, you see them on their horses, riding around doing those 'monkey drills,' pulling caissons with three-inch field pieces. If they go over, they'll be five miles behind the lines."

"Or just five hundred yards," muttered Howard.

"Yes, but they won't be in the trenches."

"They'll be in trenches."

"Yes, but not the front ones." Tommy was silent. "Howey, you've got a brain. Half these guys are hard heads from the lower East Side of New York or some farm off in the boondocks. The Artillery needs fellows with the ability to do math, algebra, figure out how to plot range, azimuths, wind velocity, things like that. You and I, we've got that ability. Why waste it? Why waste what the Army, what this country needs? We have the ability, at least the potential. We owe at least that much to our country."

Howard knew how he felt. He wanted to agree.

"I'm signing up for Artillery School in the morning," Tommy repeated.

Howard stared at him. Everything Tommy had said about being an Infantryman had been gnawing at him for the preceding ninety days. He had endured it all simply because it was an avenue to the distinction of being an "Officer and a Gentleman." How would it feel being that same "Officer and Gentleman" while riding a horse instead of slogging through the mud?

The next morning the two of them found themselves in line with a dozen other brand new Second Lieutenants, a handful of Firsts and three Captains requesting transfer to the Artillery. It took no more than ten minutes, and the two returned to their tent, quiet, delicately balancing guilt with pleasure. Over the next week, their former classmates shipped out on various assignments while the Artillery transfers quietly awaited orders to report to the Fifth Training Company.

When they took the train from Plattsburg to West Springfield for the wedding ceremony, Howard and Tommy Ross still hadn't heard.

In the best tradition of all wars, it was a military wedding. The waning sun edged over Cemetery Hill across Riverdale Street, its rays skipping over the lawn that ran down to the Connecticut River. Maude and her Springfield Girls Club urchins had covered the lawn with cotton runners from the side porch out to the minister's stand under the apple tree. As dusk settled in, she and the bridesmaids held lucifer matches to Japanese lanterns the girls had festooned over the rose arbor and out to the grape vines and apple tree branches. American flags were everywhere.

The lawn filled up with neighbors, Mount Holyoke girls, old classmates and friends over from Suffield. The Girls Club denizens grouped themselves about the lawn, sitting huddled in giggling groups, their specially designed and created dresses smearing rapidly with grass stain. Aunt Nana had arrived on the train from New York with Apsley, and George Andrews came in from Philadelphia, thoughtlessly leaving behind Howard's sister Laura.

Howard stood under the apple tree, waiting.

"Don't kiss the bride until I say 'Amen'," cautioned the good reverend, "but then do it quickly."

Eleanor Arlington glided out of the house and down the steps with Maude grasping to keep the train from snagging on the porch splinters. Only his stiff army collar kept Howard's spine from turning to jelly as his "Annabel Lee" in white crepe de chine, a shower bouquet of white roses in the crook of her arm, moved across the lawn like the angel on a Christmas tree.

Howard gave a frightened glance toward Tommy Ross, but Tommy had his eyes on Maude in the seafoam crepe with pink asters. Howard was on a runaway horse. Ellie was almost more than he could contend with. Too beautiful, too elegant, too aristocratic for a kid from Hell's Kitchen. But, as if with none of his doing, she moved gracefully to his side.

The ceremony was a blur, and the good Reverend crossed everyone up when he threw an extra "Amen" into the "Dearly Beloveds." Howard heard his cue, and pulled Ellie to him, planting a perfect score on the startled bride, a significant improvement over his dysfunctional proposal, but just a bit premature. Ellie's eyes almost popped, and everyone laughed. Howard blushed and descended to earth. It was real, and life would go on after all.

Later, Tommy was pouring the contents of a pocket flask into his glass of punch when Howard came up to the refreshment table. Tommy turned to him. "Well, old man, just like a good Artilleryman to jump the gun."

"He said to kiss her when he said 'Amen'."

"Excuses, excuses," he joked. "Have some?" He held up the now loaded glass.

From over his shoulder the voice came, "I will, if you don't mind sharing." Pa's rumpled grey sleeve cut in between the two khaki uniforms with an empty glass extended.

Howard looked quickly around for Ellie. She was sitting on the swing chatting away with C.L.I. girls. Behind them stood Ma, her eyes glued on the punch table. Her face remained impassive, but she had observed it all. Howard could say nothing.

"How about you, Howey? Want a spot?"

"No thanks, Tommy." Howard looked up at Pa, but his head was thrown back, the delicate glass pressed into his magnificent handlebar moustache that made him look so distinguished when sober and so embarrassing when not.

Pa never blinked an eye. He wiped the moustache, set the glass down on the punch table, heaved a huge sigh, turned and marched off to his little shack down by the river. Howard swung his glance over to Ma. She watched her husband all the way.

Later that evening, sober and careful, Pa drove Ellie and Howard to the Springfield train station in the Hupmobile, heading a line of cars blaring whistles and banging pans. The couple boarded a train for Rockport and the Straitsmouth Inn anticipating a two-week honeymoon. It was mid-evening when they arrived, and the bus from the Inn was waiting for them.

After dinner, Howard and Ellie sat out on the veranda while the moon moved slowly toward the west. They held hands and said very little. He found himself asking a question that had been gnawing quietly in the back of his mind.

"What happened to you and Elmore?"

When he turned to her she was staring at him. He couldn't tell if her eyes were black with fear or fury. He wanted to bite his tongue, escape the stare. It was not the question to have posed on a honeymoon.

Finally, she looked down and whispered, "I don't know."

"I'm sorry. I shouldn't have asked."

"No, it's something you should know. The problem is, I don't know the answer. And it somehow frightens me."

His mind bounced back and forth from regret to accusation, barely managing to subdue a blistering, *then why did you marry me.* Before the words could be formed, she answered.

"Howard, I don't think I ever loved Elmore."

He thanked his stars for keeping silent. For once.

She went on. "Elmore was the one everyone said I was going with. It sort of led to their saying it was going to be forever. I don't think either of us knew what to do about it. Back before you came, I used to be scared to go to school some days because I knew Elmore would be asking me to a party or to go to one of the play productions with me. Ma had to bring me hot tea in bed."

He couldn't see her eyes in the dark, but her voice was like a child's. "I was frightened, Howie. And somehow I knew you would help, save me from what I don't know, but save me from having to do what I felt everyone thought I was supposed to do. I kept saying no to you while all the time I was grateful you were there. And yet, I didn't know why you were there at all. Does that make any sense?"

"I thought you were using me." As the words tumbled out he pressed his fist to his lips. She took both his hands and pressed them to her own, and he could feel the wetness in her kiss.

"Oh, Howard, maybe I did. Maybe I did. And I'm so ashamed. But you were too good to take it that way. You were sweet, you were kind, you were brave enough to make me see what was right. I'll never forget that." And then she cried softly, saying, "And I'll always love you."

They sat quietly, holding each other. The moisture on Paradise Rocks glowed, and the salt sea smell cleared the air like a melody. Gradually they refocused on the moonlit world around them as lights in the parlor went out one by one.

"Maybe we'd better go on up." He tried to sound casual.

"All right." She moved gracefully, but very slowly. Waiting for him to lead the way?

"I have to go to the front desk to clear something up. I'll see you upstairs. Here's the key."

She looked at him briefly but turned away obediently. He went past the front desk into the bar.

"Do you have a small bottle of champagne?"

"We have half-bottles."

"Could I have one?"

"Special occasion?"

"Our honeymoon."

"Well, in that case, here's one on the house." He reached under the counter and retrieved a small green bottle of domestic. "Don't get so far gone you don't know what you're doing," he said with a wink.

Howard tucked the bottle into his front pocket where it was mostly hidden and ran up the stairs. Ellie had just arrived in the rooms and was taking her night gown from the suitcase.

"What did you have to do?"

"Nothing." He had to do better than that. "It's a surprise," he added.

Her face lit up. "I have one for you." She reached into the suitcase and brought forth a package a little more than a foot long and half as wide. She held it before him like a serving tray, wordlessly. Howard took it carefully and walked around to the side of the bed.

"What is it?"

She only beamed.

The string was simple white cord, the wrapping paper white with a silver design of bells and ribbons. The twine slipped off easily, and the wrapper unfolded to reveal an inlaid wooden box. He stared at it. Ellie reached over and unlatched the front and lifted it back on a long hinge to reveal a leather covered writing desk. In the front was a small bottle of ink on one side and a matching receptacle with paper clips on the other. She pulled on a tiny brass knob in a divider that separated the two compartments to reveal pen holders, a brush and four polished pen points.

Howard couldn't move.

"And look," Ellie went on. She pulled on a small leather strap, and up came the panel. "This is for notes and articles you're using or working on. And this"—she pulled on a leather tab inside the opened top—"this is where you put your writing paper. After you've written your short stories. And your novel," she added almost apprehensively, he thought.

The only thing that went through his mind was that he hadn't bought anything for her.

She broke the silence in a small voice. "Do you like it?"

"But I didn't get a thing for you," he answered.

"Oh, Howard." She threw her arms around him, and he could feel the tears against his cheek. "I don't want anything but you," she sobbed. They stood very still for a long while, and then they sat side-by-side on the bed looking deep into each other. Still neither spoke.

"Thank you," Howard mumbled.

She smiled. "It's really for us both, you know. The little closet there is for the notes I'm to give you for ideas and things. The big one, of course, is for what you write yourself."

They smiled some more. He mumbled "Thank you" some more. Then she rose, looked back at him and said softly, "I'm going to change.

After she closed the bathroom door, Howard took the water glasses and arranged them on the little table at the foot of the bed. Then he ducked out of his uniform into his night shirt and robe. With all that, he still had to wait several minutes before she reappeared. Howard was sitting by the little table grinning alternately at her and the little half-bottle of domestic.

"What is it? Do I look funny?" Then she caught sight of the bottle. Her expression hardly changed, but the smile inside dipped perceptibly.

"It's champagne," he explained.

"Has it got alcohol in it?"

"Yes. It's champagne." He hoped he didn't sound irritated.

She moved slowly toward the little table. "Have you tasted it?" The gown moved against her body. It was almost an afterthought to his apprehension.

"No, I was waiting for you."

She didn't answer right away. She stopped, almost by his side, staring at the little bottle, its tiny cork ensnared in a web of wire. "Well, it is our wedding, isn't it?" She seemed to be asking it of herself.

He held his breath. "Yes."

"I suppose just this once."

Howard leaped to the bottle, twisted the metal strands and eased the cork with his thumbs. Patterning his technique after the waiters he'd watched at the Cadillac Hotel while his father served as Maitre'd, he diminished the pressure on the tiny cork as he turned the bottle so that it would come out with just a tiny pop and virtually no loss of champagne. It worked. He gave Ellie a quick look for approval, not too profitable a gesture as he could tell by her worried look. Back to the task at hand, he poured the champagne into the two water tumblers very, very carefully. Howard handed her one and touched it with his own. They sipped together, eyes locked on each other's.

Ellie put a finger to her nose and grinned. "Bubbly."

"That's what they call it."

"Can't tell whether it's the bubbles or the alcohol."

"It's the bubbles," he said. "Not much alcohol in champagne."

"Really?" You could tell she wanted to believe him. He smiled and then reached around the two glasses to kiss her. She put the glass down and carefully placed her arms around his neck.

Shy? They invented the word. In the quiet, tiny room they acted out the give and take of marriage commencement with a string of muted apologies. They moved closer, acknowledging little.

The touch, the tiny sounds echoed tomb-like. Foolishly anguishing over things said and not said, couched in loneliness, he struggled between asserting and requesting. She moved hesitantly, step by step. Was she merely reflecting his uncertainty?

Reaching for the unrecognizable, still unsure, afraid to do more, but doing it nonetheless—wordlessly so as not to frighten, not to disappoint—they assumed, they assumed.

And then stillness.

The loveliness, the vision . . . jumbled images of "Annabel Lee" curled in a ball on a long, white sheet. Where have we been? What is she thinking?

His mind tumbled about. Still unsure. Still isolated.

Later in the evening, the room dark, movement lingering slowly, he heard her voice quietly ask, "You won't drink when you're in France, will you?"

Marriage, he thought, is a strange acquiescence.

Chapter Five

A phone call on the fourth day cut the honeymoon short. It was Howard's Aunt Nana in New York City.

"There's a letter here addressed to you."

"What does it say?"

"I don't know. It's from the Army, and it's addressed to you."

"You've already said that. Open it."

"It looks awfully official."

"Nana! Will you open the . . . letter!" He couldn't use Plattsburg language, but she was just the person it was designed for. He leaned on the hotel counter and waited in exasperation.

"'Dear Lieutenant Andrews, it says . . . "

"Nana, just give me the gist of it."

"Mm . . . Mm . . . you're to report on August 23rd. Howey, that's two days from now!"

"Oh, Gawd!" He got off the line as quickly as he could and rushed back to their room to pack. It was great to be starting Artillery School, but he'd just as soon finish his honeymoon.

The newlyweds caught the local to Boston, switched to the B. & A., and at Albany took the D. & H. night sleeper up to Plattsburg. There were no vacant berths, but a patriotic gentleman gave Ellie his while Howard and the gentleman sat up all night.

"Where are you stationed?"

"Plattsburgh."

"Oh, Infantry."

"Well, I was, but I put in for Artillery, and I just got word to report. We start tomorrow morning."

"Been married long?"

"A couple of days."

"You're kidding."

"No." Howard laughed. "We were just starting our honeymoon."

"Well, I'm sorry that bunk up there isn't for doubles."

Howard ducked his head and hoped he wasn't grinning too much.

In the morning, Howard turned in his Crossed Rifles for Crossed Cannons and reported to the Fifth Provisional Artillery Training Company. Tommy Ross was already signed in, but a big surprise was the appearance of old C.L.I. classmate, Ken Hall.

"Where did you come from?"

"Polly and I live in Worcester, now . . . "

"You and Polly are married?"

"Oh, yeah. We got married right after I finished Boston U. Moved over to Worcester where I'm with New England Savings. Been handling bank investments up and down the East Coast."

"Banking?" Howey speculated.

"Yes." There was a slight smile there, and Howey couldn't help detect the smugness of earlier days. It took a moment to pull himself up and go on.

"Any little Halls?"

Ken hesitated a minute, glanced at Tommy standing by, and lowered his voice. "We don't think it's right to have kids till all this is over." He glanced again at Tommy.

"Oh, I'm sorry," Howard cut in. "This is Tommy Ross. We were both reporters on the New York Sun."

"New York Sun, eh? Looks like you were doing well for yourself, Howey. Nice to meet you, Lieutenant." Ken Hall and Tommy Ross shook hands.

"Where'd you get your commission?" Howard asked.

"Fort Devon. I put in for flying, but the only thing open was Artillery spotter, so they shipped me over here for Artillery training. After we're through I'll ship to England for flying school. I hope," he added.

"Learn to ride a horse so you can handle an airplane," Tommy stuck in. "Makes sense."

"That's the Army," added Ken. They laughed.

"Where's Polly?"

"She's over at the Hostess House waiting for me to sign in."

"So's Ellie. You know Eleanor Arlington and I got married just four days ago."

"Yes, that's right! I forgot. Hey, congratulations! Ellie sent Polly an invitation, but we couldn't come because of O.C.S. Congratulations, and welcome to the club." He turned to Tommy. "You married?"

"Not me. Got more sense."

Ken Hall and Howard Andrews climbed the steps to the front porch of the Plattsburg Hostess House and two beaming brides.

"Oh, you found each other! How wonderful," Ellie bubbled slipping her arm from Polly's waist to kiss Howard's cheek.

Ken pulled Polly in close and put his free hand out for Ellie. "Congratulations, Ellie, and our really sincere apologies for missing the wedding."

"I told her you were getting that funny little gold thing on your collar," Polly interjected with a giggle.

"Well, we certainly would have been there," Ken added. "And, Howey, I can't tell you how much we admire your . . . " he seemed to be scrambling for just the right phrase . . . "good taste and perseverance." He and Polly grinned. "I hope you appreciate what a good match you've made for yourself."

Howard had a flashback to the days when he sat at the back of the class at the Connecticut Literary Institute, quite apart from New England's gentry. But then, just as he had once fixed his eyes on the willowy school girl with the black-ribband braids, he turned again to Ellie and gently pulled her to his side.

The two couples teamed up to find a place outside camp for the wives. A Methodist Minister named Dr. Meade offered two rooms, and within hours the girls were unpacked and filling in the gaps that seven years had left in their lives.

Like Eleanor Arlington, Polly and Ken Hall were old New England stock, genteel and a bit grand. Even Polly, for all her buxom effervescence, carried herself with an air of importance. Ken even more so, for his was a family that went back to 1637 when Isaac Hall settled in West Suffield. The Halls even had a street named after them. None of this could be matched by the rough and tumble background of Howard Andrews and Tommy Ross back in New York. Yet Howard felt a New England marriage and an Army commission gave him a foot in gentility's door, uneasily perhaps, but it was a circumstance he was most amenable to and by most rights felt he'd earned.

Tommy Ross and ties to the NY Sun began to fade from the picture. With the Halls, Howey had eased into Suffield society.

Polly was a godsend for Ellie. On the front porch of the Hostess House across from Post Headquarters parade ground, they watched their husbands drill, deploy up and down the common, and stand formation before the flagpole. They watched in amusement while the candidates, some of them city boys like Howard, hitched and drove six-horse battery teams hauling three-inch field pieces and caissons off to the New York State hills.

On weekends, the new foursome walked the hills, explored the town of Plattsburg, took pictures of each other, girls in long skirts and blouses with pilgrim collars, men in broad-brimmed, high, crown-pinched hats, hip-length buttoned blouses, billowing breeches and legs canvas-calved with "puttees," strutting like roosters, holding the girls as they balanced on railroad tracks, beaming for the Kodak.

Howard took the camera as Ken walked the girls up the tracks, treading the ties while they held his hands and balanced on the rails. Through the lens, Howard gleamed at Ellie's trim figure moving away with delicate grace. His eyes shifted onto the shorter, bulkier, full-bosomed Polly, noting the way her hips swung right and left with the precision of a well shaped-mare. He found himself wondering how they would respond beneath . . . .

Ken turned around, and the girls pivoted on the rails, releasing his hands and then grabbing them intently to stay aloft, Ellie so careful, Polly so abandoned, her blouse bulging and spreading the lapels of her fall suit . . . .

Ellie hopped from the rail and rushed to take the camera. "You two stand over there by the stone lion. No, not you, Polly, just Howey and Ken."

Howard positioned himself before the statuary in a three-quarter pose overlapping the more pliant Ken Hall. Together, they fixed frozen smiles. And waited.

"What's the matter?"

"Where do you look?"

"In the little lens on the top. The little piece of glass."

"There's one on the top and one on the side."

"Which way are you taking it?"

"I'm taking it of you."

Howard broke his pose. "I mean are you taking it horizontally or vertically?"

"What does that mean?"

He lunged toward her and reached for the camera. "Give me the damn thing."

Her eyes flashed from the Kodak onto his, hands locking the camera at her waist. Howard gestured for it impatiently.

"What was that word?"

Howard paled at her cold tone.

"What word?"

"You know the word I mean. Don't use that word with me, Howey."

He murmured, "I didn't mean anything. I just wanted to show you."

Slowly she handed him the camera.

Laughter came with difficulty throughout the rest of the day. In the dark of bedroom night she turned to whisper, "I'm sorry I embarrassed you this afternoon. You should have taken a hairbrush to me."

He didn't know how to answer. Why would she apologize for his indiscretion? It was an uncomfortable escape.

Having someone just his own was an uneasy godsend. All guarantees were gone. There was no consistency, no sureness in marriage. There were unexpected turns, her face on entering a room, the frightened look mysteriously disappearing into an unexplainable smile. A sublime mirage, like Douglas Fairbanks and Mary Pickford on a black and white screen. Uncertainties everywhere, some frightening, but some, oh, some so glorious and giving that it seemed he had climbed up onto that screen with America's sweetheart.

While the future Artillery officers learned how men would fire three-inch field pieces, cold wind from the Great Lakes pummeled Plattsburg, and September moved into October, November. Off base, the officers switched to long olive-drab coats with huge collars and leather-peaked caps adorned with metallic insignia pinned above the bill, and the ladies disappeared into long cloth coats with lambs wool collars, wrist-deep in muffs, all black. Hats materialized out of nowhere, some pork-pied, some broad-brimmed like the officers' summer ones, but feather-decorated and rakish, still in black.

"Get your hands off that pommel, Lieutenant!"

Howard's horse ambled along, sidling to the left and to the right as he nudged the beast around the tent pegs planted twenty feet apart.

"Cross those arms! Use your knees, use your butt! Lean! Lean, Lieutenant!" The training sergeant obviously enjoyed his job.

Plattsburg's Fifth Training Company included some of the best riders in the country. Internationally-known polo players, now uniformed, guided their intelligent beasts by imperceptible shifting of leg and seat. Experts who had to have come from circuses did "monkey drills," standing in the saddle astride four horses and climbing in dizzy pyramids at full gallop. Howard and most of the Fifth Training Company were newcomers to horse drawn artillery. They were city boys who didn't know a caisson from a milk wagon.

Fall of 1917 moved into a bitter winter, and cold winds from the St. Lawrence whipped through canvas tents. Horses snorted dripping vapor, shot acrid streams of urine and dropped steaming heaps of dung throughout the frozen parade ground. The prospect of France began to loom as a promise of relief.

In late November Tommy Ross ran through camp waving his orders and laughing like a loon. He had been assigned to an air school in England for training as an aero-communications officer, an artillery spotter, the very job Ken Hall had asked for and anticipated. It was Tommy Ross, not Ken Hall, who would be the flyer.

Ken Hall was stunned. "You're going *where*?"

"To England! I'm gonna fly an aeroplane! Me, an artillery spotter! Ain't that the hots?"

Ken's expression never changed. "'Ours is not to reason why'," he paraphrased. But his head tilted back slightly, and his jaw muscles pumped as he turned back to study his own notice of assignment.

Howard was only somewhat envious. He wasn't sure he wanted to fly those "jennys."

"Where are you going, Howey?"

"Ken and I are going to Camp Meade."

Tommy looked quizzical for a minute. "What outfit?"

"The 351st Field Artillery."

"My God, that's the 'Buffalo' Division. The 92nd. It's a jigaboo outfit!" And he roared with laughter. "Hey, gang, Howey and Ken are gonna go boom-boom with a bunch of coons!"

Howard and Ken stared at each other, but Ken's face remained stolid. Howard's mind snapped back to ragged West Side gangs racing down Tenth Avenue, the Cadillac Hotel, the face-offs, the backing-down, the words mumbled as backs were turned, Boudreau's grin and the swinging door slapping back and forth.

Ken murmured stiffly, "Tennyson wrote the rules. 'Ours is not to reason why'," he repeated. Then he concluded: "'ours is but to do or die'."

"' . . . do *and* die'," Howard corrected.

Ken stared blankly a moment and then responded, "Either-or."

Tommy Ross was on the next train to New York and the next ship to England. Howard wondered if—or when—he'd be shot down.

A week later, the two married couples boarded a similar train, this one for Baltimore. With them were half-a-dozen other shavetails, some also with wives whose arms threaded their own and disappeared in huge, furry muffs. They said goodbye to friends, to other wives, to marriage cots. All sat upright till the coach stopped hours later in Maryland.

From a platform in the middle of downtown Baltimore, Enrico Caruso, live and in person—not an acoustical platter turning on a table, but Enrico, himself—serenaded the new arrivals with George M. Cohan's "Over There." Down below, mingling within the crowds, Charlie Chaplin and Mary Pickford sold War Bonds.

Howard and his bride wove through the star struck crowd and trudged through Baltimore snowdrifts looking for a place for Ellie to live.

Chapter Six

Mrs. Stewart and her two prim, Civil-War-bred daughters offered board and lodging for a modest consideration extended to officers' wives only. The matriarch hesitated a bit when asked to take in a girl from Massachusetts because she had been raised to believe that all denizens of that Commonwealth bore horns and a tail. She had been more than forty before discovering that "damn Yankee" was not one word.

"I understand your lovely wife plays the piano," cooed Miss May, Mrs. Stewart's youngest daughter, the one who kept licking the mole on her upper lip. She was only fifty-two.

"Yes, Ma'am. She's very good."

"Perhaps you'll honor us after dinner," drawled her sister Asa with the scraggly curls in front of each ear and the eyebrows fused together. She was fifty-five.

"I'll be happy to," answered Ellie.

Dishes had been set and cleared by a coal-black woman in her sixties. As Mrs. Stewart led the procession into the parlor, she announced regally that "Miss Noolie" had been with her for fifty-seven years.

"She was my wedding present when she was just a 'pickaninny' and has been with me ever since." With the briefest pause, she added, "despite the War of Northern Aggression."

Ellie sat before the ivory keys and carefully opened a music book on the rack. "What would you like to hear?"

"I'd love to hear 'Nearer My God to Thee'," cooed Miss May with a nimble flick of the tongue.

Ellie played to the end.

"Do you know 'Jesus, I Come?'" drawled Miss Asa, the older one, her eyebrows rising in the middle.

Howard stifled a gulp.

"I don't believe I know that," Ellie answered discreetly.

"It's in the book," commanded Mrs. Stewart.

Ellie leafed through it and found the obscure selection. She carefully and gently fingered the first few chords to acclimate herself as the ancient lady added:

"It's one of our most beautiful Southern hymns. It tells how we feel about the Lord."

Howard leaned to tighten his shoe laces.

Miss Noolie appeared and poured five tiny glasses of sherry. Then, after placing them on a small, silver tray, she offered one to Mrs. Stewart who raised a finger and nodded toward Ellie. The silent black figure moved slipper-like to the piano where Ellie was finishing the hymn.

Ellie glanced down at the tray, blanched and then caught Howard's empty expression before shaking her head, murmuring "No, thank you."

Miss Noolie turned to her mistress, eyes searching for instructions. A light wave of the head and a nod toward the source of the wine told Noolie to remove the still filled glasses and depart. And that she did.

After a slight downtrodden look toward Howard, Ellie returned to the keys. Howard avoided looking at the ladies who appeared ready to go on forever, sherry or no sherry, but Mrs. Stewart cranked herself up out of the chair and headed through the draped portico for the next room. Ellie continued to play. Mrs. Stewart stopped and turned by the portieres.

"What, pray tell . . . is that?"

Ellie stopped, startled at the abruptness. "It's rag."

"It's what?"

"Ragtime. I heard it at Mount Holyoke. I believed it was Southern," she added hesitantly.

"This is Sunday, m'dear, and we allow only hymns to be played on the Lord's Day," Mrs. Stewart intoned. "That or 'Maryland, My Maryland.' And we certainly do not allow Nehgrah music in our home." She pronounced "our" with two distinct syllables.

Asa and May worried their handkerchiefs while Howard glanced around the room grasping for a mode of retreat.

"How the hell are you going to survive in this house?"

"Howard!" Ellie scowled, laying the Saturday Evening Post on the bed sheet beside her. He could see the glint behind the frown. "Your language!"

"Honey, these people will eat you alive." He paused to listen for footsteps outside their bedroom door. "I don't see how we ever won the war."

"Howey, she's just a dear, sweet little old lady."

"And the girls? Especially that one with the mole . . . and the tongue!"

"We don't call them girls, dear. They're young ladies."

"Honey, they're twice our age."

"Howey, we're in the South, now. You know what they say about 'doing in Rome'."

"Well . . . " He paced around the room a few times, stopping to look out the window at the Baltimore thoroughfare. Snow was falling gently, street lights made yellowish pools on the white blanket, and house lights turned all into a Christmas card scene. In reality, however, it was just simply cold. Howard knew it, felt it. Wet and cold.

Christmas came with a difference. Four days leave with Ellie's family back in Springfield. Snowballs, sledding down Witch's Path from Cemetery Hill, a family whose warmth cut through the winter. In the evenings, Pa and Ma read in the living room, Pa in the big chair, his tobacco stand beneath the window and the floor lamp between, lighting playing cards on the solitaire board balanced on the wide, flat, wooden arm rests, a palm-grip curve near the end. Ma sat in a straight-back beside the little center table with its own lamp, squinting through bi-focals at the stitching in her sampler. Behind, the floor furnace snapped on and off, crackling with the changing temperatures. Maude played piano in the parlor.

Howard and Ellie retreated to the little back room upstairs where Pa was occasionally confined when he got too drunk. Howard read and sketched while Ellie sewed. She pulled the dresser drawer open and stopped still a moment, closing her eyes.

"You're all right?"

"No, I'm fine."

What does that mean? *Fine* means she's all right. *No*, she's not? He couldn't understand, stared at her, head buried in one of the dresser drawers.

"You looking for something?"

"The darning ball."

"The marble one, the egg?"

"No, the wooden one with the handle. Never mind. Here it is."

As she straightened up she winced. Her hand was in the middle of her back when she turned around, and she drew air through her teeth.

"You all right?"

"I'm all right."

The pain seemed to leave as though it had never touched her. She threaded the needle, thrust the wooden ball into a khaki sock and carefully wove the strand over a bare spot. He waited. She had to sense the waiting.

Her lips moved in and out like they sometimes did on the corners of his mouth, and then her eyes popped up onto his as though they were joined at the orbs. And her mouth no longer could hold back the smile.

"I think we're going to have a little stranger."

What was she talking about? She laughed as if he were a little boy. Just the way he felt.

"You're going to be a father."

And then she laughed outright.

The abandonment within that laugh darted about the room like a loose artillery round. In a strange, massive way, he felt uncertainty and constraint invading their relationship, her ties—her obligation—to him and to him alone.

Ken had said it. *Why bring children into a world at war?* Why bring children at all? Children were the consequence of marriage, yes, but mothers left children. Mothers left husbands.

Would he be like his father?

George Andrews, Howard's father, had been Maitre d' at the old Cadillac Hotel on Ninth and Forty-Second from the time he arrived out of Glasgow on December 11, 1882 till the day he became a book salesman. The time Baby Laura and then six-year-old Howard had climbed onto the famous "Diamond Jim" Brady knee where Howard actually fingered the famous diamonds, that time floated close to the surface of Howard's memory pool.

"My God, the little devil's after m'diamonds!" Brady had roared.

George Andrews' arbitrary yank that sent his frightened son across the dining room with a cuff ringing in his ear was only part of the memory. The dining room laughter and his father's grin and wagging finger added a secondary insult to injury.

But Boudreau, the little Haitian boy who lugged dirty plates to a line of kitchen dishwashers—"pearl-divers," hotel people called them—had completed the little drama, for little Boudreau had marched stolidly over to the illustrious lap, climbed aboard and neatly removed the hugely adorned stickpin from Brady's ascot. Instead of a cuff on the ear, Boudreau got a silver coin as a swap along with a round of applause that carried him back through the swinging kitchen doors where the "pearl-divers" ogled and gaped. Boudreau's glance at Howard telegraphed his message:

"That's how you handle rich folks, White Boy," it seemed to say.

"Nigger bastard!" hissed Howard. Boudreau's answer was the kitchen door slapping back and forth, but the flared nostrils and the dark brown smile linked him forever to the stinging blow ringing in Howard's left ear.

When the Baptist Church on New York's West 66th Street sent fifteen-year-old Howard to Suffield, he took with him a bitterness born out of what he termed indifferent and calloused parents plus the rough give-and-take of the Melting Pot. Along with all this came the labels acquired in Hell's Kitchen. He could recite them one by one: "Wop, dago, spade, square-head, jew-boy, polack, nigger, lily-white, coon, chink, mick, kike, jigaboo, slant-eyes, shade, shine," and more—tags that separated true Americans from the riff-raff.

Unlike Hell's Kitchen, Suffield was "lily white." Even the ex-slaves had moved out after the Civil War. Not even "polacks" and "shanty-Irish" inhabited Suffield. Suffield was white, English, middle class farm people, not Hell's Kitchen hovel.

But vocabulary had not been the challenge in Howard's shift to Suffield. No, instead it had been the bitter realization that an orphan from Hell's Kitchen wore the same kind of label in Suffield that Boudreau had worn in the Cadillac Hotel. That's what had bothered him. He became like the boy in the story who carried a baby fox to school and stoically endured the gnawing under his jacket for fear of revealing the beast. Hell's Kitchen was Howard's beast, and no matter how he tried to hide it, the beast gnawed at his core.

All America knew that Germany's Kaiser had scoffed at slave descendants ever fighting for their country, that in 1917 General "Blackjack" Pershing had ordered a Negro division formed, the 92nd Division, nicknamed "The Buffalo Division" after the earlier "Buffalo Soldiers." They were given a patch with the black silhouette of an American buffalo on a field of brown with a black border. Cooks and road workers were pulled out of camps all over the south. Every Negro who could "shoot and salute" became an infantryman. The "Buffalo" Division went into the front line with black enlisted men and white officers, graded, commissioned and baptized in record time, and Pershing thumbed his nose at the Kaiser.

Howard's arrival at Camp Meade's Artillery Brigade Headquarters had been a reversal from his arrival in Suffield. The 351st Regiment was all black, yes, but, my God, in Hell's Kitchen there had been some parity. Here he was outnumbered! And black troops firing three-inch field pieces? My God, less than sixty years before, Ellie's landlady had been given a "pickaninny" as her wedding present!

Howard and Ken Hall had reported to the Battery Commander together, their wives left to the vagaries of isolated Baltimore Boarding Houses.

"Relax, Lieutenants." He pulled on his right ear lobe as he scanned two papers before him to determine which was which. "You're Hall, I gather," he ventured, looking up at Ken.

"Yes, Sir."

"That makes you Andrews."

"Yes, Sir," Howard answered smartly.

"I'm Captain Lewis and this is my Administrative Officer, Lieutenant Foot."

A leathery First Lieutenant with a Texas accent and a large cigar wedged between piano-keyed teeth leaned in and shook hands. As he did, a fresh faced Second Lieutenant raced through the door apologizing.

"Sorry I'm late. Hi! Hi! I'm O'Reilly, Third Platoon Leader."

Howard took his hand and said slyly, "Oh, really?"

The Lieutenant came back like a whip, "No! O'Reilly."

The two of them laughed, and Lieutenant Foot roared. Ken stared for a moment before joining in half heartedly. Captain Lewis looked up as though he'd missed something.

"O'Reilly and Foot have been running this company with me the last three months," Lewis went on, "so we're glad to get up to strength at last. Foot had your platoon, Hall, so he can fill you in. I moved him up to Administration and Supply which God knows we've needed. Andrews, your platoon's been on its own, but you'll find you've got one of the best sergeants in the Battalion so you shouldn't have any trouble."

"Lt. Andrews?"

"Yes, Sergeant?"

The sergeant was shorter than Howard, about thirty pounds heavier with shoulders and biceps that stretched his wool O.D. shirt. His hair was glued down with pomade, and he spoke quietly with a slight French accent. But the full-lipped smile that broke over his face shocked Howard back to Hell's Kitchen the Cadillac Hotel . . . and the lap of "Diamond Jim" Brady.

"What's your name, Sergeant?"

"Sergeant Boudreau," and there was a perceptible pause before the added, "Sir."

The Sergeant reported the platoon ready for inspection, stepped back smartly, saluted and executed a perfect, military about-face before moving to his position at the right of the platoon.

That momentary silent stare had followed mutual recognition and had validated their newfound relationship. That sign of shared recollection was to be their last, for neither ever mentioned "Diamond Jim" Brady or the kitchen of the Cadillac Hotel dining room with its swinging doors brushing aside Howard's stinging, "Nigger bastard!" Boudreau the little Haitian "pearl-diver" was now strapping Sergeant Boudreau and, as the Captain said, "one of the best sergeants in the Battalion."

Chapter Seven

Something was happening to Howard. But he wasn't quite sure what it was. Or even if it was really happening or not. It's just that two words kept drifting into his consciousness. Or "barging" was a more likely term. He just couldn't fathom why they were there or what they signified. He knew what they were: one was "responsibility," and the other was "command." Sometimes they came to him in combined form as "Command Responsibility" but most often as two separate words.

"Responsibility" he had grown up with, responsibility to others, his father, the employers, to the teachers at C.L.I. and, above all, to himself. He'd been taught to be responsible for everything he did. It restricted him, and he didn't like it, but he obeyed dutifully. He obeyed the law of "responsibility."

"Command" was something new—if one discounted the "commands" laid upon him by his father, along with society and its bullies. Its current form first appeared during those training sessions on Governor's Island. It grew in strength and significance as he and his fellow Officer Candidates moved to Plattsburg, and it grew also as a measure of support and reliability, things he'd never before felt were a part of his life. Command bespoke The Army, and he liked it.

Now he was a bearer as well as a recipient of these two things, Responsibility and Command. He found that, with his platoon of thirty-six men, four of them Squad Leaders and one a Platoon Sergeant—yes, and Sgt. Boudreau—the two words had settled into a new and compelling sequence of sounds. It was now "Command Responsibility." He liked that. It lent nobility. It gave him purpose, an agenda and, for the first time in his life, the opportunity for largess. Not from others, but from him. He could grant. He could allow. He could bestow. He might be only a lowly Second Lieutenant, but he had Command and Responsibility over thirty-six men. And the mantle rested easily on his eager and receptive shoulders.

At the same time, Howard's life had gradually divided itself into three distinct areas. To each he tried to apply his new-found regimen of Command Responsibility.

For the Army, that was simple, for his platoon was "present and accounted for," while the Company Commander, Executive Officer, Battalion Staff, Regiment and on up were all pre-ordained. All he had to do was recognize and obey.

His career took a little more thought because it was, perforce, on hold. He'd scribbled things and tucked them away in the writing desk kept protected, wrapped in a woolen army blanket, from the day he and Ellie had moved out of Plattsburg for Ft. Meade. There wasn't much in it: a patch work diary of sorts, a few helter-skelter observations on Army life, the unfinished efforts of a Saturday Evening Post story and even an article or two he'd written for his old boss at The New York Sun but never got the nerve to send. But he did have a plan, a goal. It would go into effect the moment he was on his way to the Front. He would be a combat correspondent who really was in combat. The old boss would surely see the significance in this. It was a shoe-in. Next would come the real stories—they were sure to come once he was in France—the stories that *Liberty* would gobble up and even the *Post.* He would even offer sketches or maybe water colors to illustrate his stories. He would be both author and artist. Everything was there. All that was needed was time and circumstance. He had the "responsibility"—it was to his talent—and he had the "command"—which was his talent, itself. "Command Responsibility!" The words came together, just like in the Army. Or so it seemed.

And the third element? Ah, the third! It was hard to say, to speak the word, to accept it as one of the three great challenges of his life, to say it openly, the "responsibility" or the "command" for—marriage!

He'd tried "command" once: "Give me the damn thing." And he saw quickly what that turned into. He'd hid "responsibility" in his monthly pay check, in carrying suitcases and opening doors, in behavior as "An Officer And A Gentleman." But in marriage the two words were still separate. They didn't come together easily in marriage as they did with the other two concerns. And they certainly didn't come in the same sequence. It was "Responsibility" and then "command"—with a small "c."

Still, "Command Responsibility" was Howey's new mantra, and if he couldn't apply it successfully to all three venues in his new life, then he would have to let time bend the venues to this new order of things. He would study marriage.

He would study marriage as he had studied the Army. He would set his marriage in order as he had been setting his career in order. He would study, read about it, learn from those who know. He would learn about marriage from the experts, just as one learns from great writers and superior officers. And he would apply this learning to his native intelligence. Yes, that was it! His native intelligence! He wasn't Hell's Kitchen detritus any more. He wasn't an abandoned orphan at C.L.I. He was "An Officer And A Gentleman," and there was a way. There was a way because there was a will, and where there was a will there was a way. He almost grinned as he thought through the words.

"Now, let's get on with this war," he added.

Chapter Eight

Sergeant Boudreau was the best. Spit and polish, he was at the ready whenever Howard turned around. The men lined up each morning, squads snapping to attention when the Platoon Leader marched up.

"All present and accounted for, Sir," snapped the sergeant.

"Move out," snapped the lieutenant.

Boudreau marched the men to the gun emplacement, and the men began their ever-expanding affair with three-inch towed-mounts.

"Hey, Howey."

"Ken."

"Have you got an orderly yet?

"No. I haven't pushed it. I figured I'd let Sergeant Boudreau check out the platoon for a volunteer."

Lieutenant Ken Hall was as nervous as a kitten, a Connecticut Yankee isolated from his all-white society. But Howard had a leg-up. Being from the West Side had its advantages. Howard would help

Ken and the other officers get along with the all-Negro 351st and be top dog in no time. He could even see himself commanding a company of his own.

"Don't worry, Ken. I'll work out something so you'll have an orderly."

"Well, I've already got a candidate in my platoon, but I was hoping you might share him with me. Can't afford more than five clams, and most of the officers are doubling up so the orderlies can make more money."

Howard huffed a bit. "Where is he?"

"Over with my platoon. I'll send him to you during a break."

"What's your name, soldier?"

"ChewSAH."

"Very good, but don't forget the 'Sir' when you're speaking to an officer."

"I did, SAH! My name's Chew . . . C-H-E-W, Sah!"

Chew got ten dollars added to his Buck Private's thirty, a good income. Lieutenants Howard Andrews and Kenneth Hall had the shiniest boots, the biggest meals and the hottest baths in the field thanks to Private Chew . . . SAH!

Captain Lewis, Battery Commander, gave his new officers a week to settle in. Four days, to be exact. Four days of gun drill, close order drill, calisthenics and policing the area. On Friday, he pulled all four lieutenants into his office for a surprise assignment. The Battalion Commander had begun to lay on all the full weight of Advanced Training, and Captain Lewis was passing along the good news.

"Now that we've got this Battery up to full strength," the captain growled, pulling on his earlobe, "the Old Man has some fancy projects for us." He gestured to the Platoon Leaders arrayed before him. "You, Hall, are to take your platoon out to the south end of the firing range and build a gun emplacement for a Three-Inch Towed Mount, you, O'Reilly, one for a Howitzer and, Andrews, you got the fancy job of constructing a radio tower."

"A what?"

"A radio tower. You know, an antenna."

"How high?"

"I don't know. Thirty feet. High enough to receive signals from Meade Headquarters."

"Where am I supposed to get that sort of pole?"

"That's your problem. That's why we're supposed to do these crazy things, to show how smart we are, how we can get along with nothing, go to France and win this war."

Lieutenant Foot tilted his chair back against the wall, grinning as he chewed on his cigar, and rubbed his Texas-baked neck. After savoring the confusion, he suggested the three officers might find some help in his supply tent.

"Shovels, wire, sand bags, planks. Even got some one-by-threes you might wire together and stretch out into a pole," he offered slyly.

"Start Monday. Use the weekend to figure out how you're going to do this, check out your locations and look over what Foot's got in his Supply tent. That's all." The three Platoon Leaders straggled out warily without even a nod to the frazzled Captain Lewis and his grinning Assistant Commanding Officer.

"You guys got it easy," growled Howard. "All you got to do is fill sand bags and haul a piece into firing position. How the hell am I going to make a radio tower?" Ken Hall and Lyons stared blankly.

Howard caught Sergeant Boudreau just outside the Mess Hall, filling him in on the unpleasant details. "You have any idea how we can build a radio tower out of one-by-three planks?" he groused.

"No, but I can get you a flag pole."

Howard stared at him. "You're kidding! Where?"

With a wily glance about, Boudreau described the Meade supply and ordinance depot hidden in one of the far corners of the camp. It was completely accessible around midnight!

Howard nixed that. "We're supposed to use only the stuff we get from Lieutenant Foot's supply tent."

Boudreau shrugged his shoulders saying offhand, "Well, if you want it built . . . that's one way to get it done."

"Well, it's not our way. We're going to do this by the book. No stealing."

"It's called Midnight Requisitioning, Lieutenant. And it's the Army way."

Howard thought carefully before he spoke. "You filch that flag pole, Sergeant, and you won't get two bits and a round of applause."

The sergeant dipped his head slightly, touched his right forefinger to his brow and stepped back before wheeling and marching into the Mess Hall. Howard couldn't tell if Boudreau was seething or laughing at him.

Howard made his own way to the Camp bus stop, mulling over the impossible task before him, wondering if he'd done the right thing. The smart thing. The responsible thing.

That night, after a chilly dinner at the Stewarts', Howard stared out the bedroom window at tree-lined Baltimore, its snowy skirts whirling in the wind.

"What's the matter, honey?"

He couldn't tell Ellie that he was worried about something as foolish as building an antenna. All weekend he had ground thoughts to a dust and blown them from his mind, one miserable prospect after another. He knew Ellie was placating him, deferring to his moods, and it only irritated him more.

Monday morning came too quickly. It ended a miserable weekend, and it brought no solution to the monster looming on his conscience. Ellie's last words startled him.

"Don't worry, honey, everything will be all right."

He hadn't realized he'd been that transparent. *Perhaps that is good*, he thought. *She should know the hell I have to go through. This will be good*, he kept telling himself. *Let her know how much responsibility I've shouldered.* He waved to her through the bus window. *This will be good*, he mulled over and over.

The day was spent with squad leaders taking the men through calisthenics and close order drill while Howard and Platoon Sergeant Boudreau rummaged through the pitiful stock of goods in Lt. Foot's Supply tent. They found wire and tent pegs, but there was nothing longer than a six foot plank to make the antenna. In every movement of Boudreau's shoulders Howard could sense the sergeant's underlying contention that there was a flag pole, just waiting to be "requisitioned."

By the end of the day, they had accumulated three bales of wire, one box of tent pegs, five hammers, a bag of six-penny nails . . . and a small stack of low grade, yellow pine, one-by-threes, each a measly six feet long.

Sergeant Boudreau threw Lieutenant Andrews a soft salute as they went their separate ways for that evening's chow call. Howard struggled with his depression and the gnawing realization that, though he, himself, may be right, Boudreau was the clever one. After picking over his meal, Howard plodded back to the Officers Quarters and lay on his bunk, hands clasped behind his head, mentally nailing, wrapping in wire lengthy triangles of pine planks, and stretching them into a thirty-foot pole. He could see them collapsing in a mass of splintered wood and wire. He lay, lonely, his misery finally interrupted by a tap on the door frame.

"Excuse me, Sir, but Private Chew has got hisself into a bit of trouble, Sir." Sergeant Boudreau stood in the doorway of the B.O.Q. cubicle, right hand to his eyebrow. "Lieutenant Hall felt you might want to know that Chew might not be out of the infirmary tomorrow."

"What happened?"

"Well, Sir, there'd been a bit of a ruckus in the shower, and he kind of got the worst of it."

Over Boudreau's shoulder, Howard could see Ken Hall lumbering down the hallway, chuckling as he came. "You hear about Chew?" Ken called.

"Sergeant Boudreau is just telling me."

Ken shook his head and glanced briefly at the sergeant as if to check before going on. "You know Chew takes a ribbing like all orderlies, but he's a Georgia field hand," he rambled on, "black as a black cat at midnight in a coal bin with no moon, and he got an extra dose in the showers last night."

"What happened?"

"Well, the way I hear it, he was standing there naked when someone asked him if he was gettin' sick. Told him he was getting a tad pale lately. My Platoon Sergeant told them to let the boy alone . . . told them nothing was the matter except a little touch of white blood in him. Chew jumped both of them."

As Ken burst out laughing, Howard tried not to look at Boudreau. "Orderlies take a lot of ribbing," he echoed.

"Especially when they're as black as Chew," Ken added with a loud guffaw.

Boudreau didn't join in on the laugh. He measured Lieutenant Hall coldly.

"Maybe the Lieutenant would prefer I find him a white orderly, one who looked more like the Lieutenant." Even in his soft, lyrical, Haitian dialect the Sergeant's words bit harshly.

Ken stared at the Sergeant.

Howard could almost see the wheels turning in Ken's head, the flashing resentment struggling against inbred abnegation, self-criticism, the years of innocence. Howard's own reaction was more in keeping with Hell's Kitchen and the fury that engulfed him that day in the Cadillac Hotel.

"Get your platoon together, Sergeant. You've got a transmission center to build first thing in the morning," Howard snapped.

Sergeant Boudreau threw a salute, very military. Howard could almost feel the ripple of his muscles as the sergeant pivoted and plodded off, pounding heels echoing through the shadowy hallway.

"Sorry about that," he muttered to Ken.

"Jesus! I didn't know I'd said anything . . . . " Ken's voice trailed off.

The next morning, Howard went through the motions of chow call, stuffing down grits, dry scrambled eggs and black coffee, dreading the meeting with his platoon, tackling the impossible, a tower made of wood scraps! He found himself approaching the parade grounds, aware that he hadn't raised his eyes from his shoelaces since leaving the mess hall.

Off in the corner where his platoon should have been lined up in formation with Sergeant Boudreau in front at Parade Rest, was a strange gathering at the center of which stood Lieutenant Foot, Captain Lewis and—if his eyes weren't deceiving him—Major Clifton Harris, the Battalion Commander, Major Harris. The Major was smiling, one arm extended his way in as close to an embrace as a Commanding Commanding Officer might be expected to offer.

"Great job, Lieutenant! How'd you get it done so fast? And where'd you get the pole? Fantastic."

Howard was aghast. Rising high above the Parade Ground—at least thirty feet!—was the tallest flag pole he'd ever seen, struts of wire extending in four directions from its midsection and top to tent pegs arranged in giant squares. And crowned at the top was a metal rod that trailed a long wire over to an olive drab, folding field table.

"Where'd you get the pole, Lieutenant?" repeated Major Harris.

"The Sergeant . . . ," Howard began, looking over at Boudreau staring at him, one eyebrow slightly elevated, an inscrutable half-smile on his lips.

"Sergeant, did you do this?" Major Harris went on, cheerfully.

"Oui, Sir."

"And speaks French, too," roared the Major, bursting with laughter. "You got yourself a gold mine, Lieutenant. You're going to have it rough hanging on to this fellow." He looked long and hard at Boudreau, all the while nodding to himself.

Sergeant Boudreau avoided looking at his Platoon Leader, but the avoidance was mutual. The rest of the day was spent testing out the antenna with battalion radio equipment. Boudreau did most of the testing, but he was obviously careful to make sure his Platoon Leader was kept up to snuff on all matters.

In the days that followed, rumors circulated that seven Non-Coms were being sent to Artillery Officer's Candidate School. With the rumor came disbelief and a lot of scoffing. Enlisted Men were black, Officers were white. That's the way "Blackjack" Pershing had set it up. Blacks would never go to Officer's Candidate School.

Early Wednesday morning, Howard headed for the Parade Grounds to take over his platoon, but in Sergeant Boudreau's place was an ex-clerk ten years Boudreau's senior. There was no warning, no farewell, no best wishes. When Howard turned up at Captain Lewis' office that evening, the Captain apologized.

"Oh, Gawd, Howey, I just got so busy I forgot. Last night, Regiment sent down orders for Negro candidates. Evidently Major Harris, the Battalion Commander, didn't waste much time making a choice, considering your antenna marvel. I had to have Boudreau up at Regiment by seven this morning." He paused.

Howard offered no response. The Captain asked, "How's the new sergeant make out?"

"Just fine," Howard murmured as he turned to leave. As far as he was concerned, that was as much as the C. O. deserved.

Chapter Nine

Ellie lay on both pillows propped against the headboard thumbing through the magazine. "Have you read this installment in the 'Post'?"

"No."

Howard watched her from the far side of the room. A few brief treasured hours, a balance between structured politeness with the Stewarts and warm closeness in the huge bed, second floor front. He valued his Wednesday nights away from Meade even more than the weekends, especially now that Ellie was expecting. He couldn't be sure there was any sign of Buddy yet, but he'd begun to notice a little something when she slipped into her nightgown. He still couldn't get over how pretty she was.

"What's the matter? Why are you looking at me?"

"Nothing." He turned back to the window. She was still staring at him when he looked back. "You really look . . . nice," he muttered.

She smiled. He grinned back at her.

Ellie lay the Saturday Evening Post on the bed table and patted the covers beside her. "Come here."

Howard half reclined on his side of the bed. She took his hand and moved it over to where Buddy was making himself known.

"Feel anything?"

"No."

"Just wait."

They waited. Together. But Buddy wasn't cooperating.

"I'm anxious for him to get here."

"Or her," he cautioned.

"Oh, no. It's our Buddy, and he'll be christened Howard G. Andrews, Junior."

Parenthood, like marriage, was a growing amalgam of celebration and imposition. Command and Responsibility, but more Responsibility than Command, the way it was turning out.

It was another Wednesday evening. Howard found Ellie curled up on the bed, lights out, eyes wide open.

"You all right?"

"Yes."

"Last time we had this conversation you announced you were pregnant."

She rolled over and smiled. "Same story," she said.

He moved in beside her. "What's the matter?"

"Oh, I don't want to complain. It's just difficult being here alone all day. I've been a little sick to my stomach." She want on after a pause. "The Stewarts are really very nice, but . . . "

Howard knew what she was thinking. "Honey, it won't be long. We'll be going across soon, I'm sure. And then you can go back to Springfield."

"Oh, Howey, can't I go back now!" Her eyes were flooding over. He wanted to give in, but the thought was suffocating.

"Honey, I can't bear the idea of you being anywhere on this continent and not with me," he pleaded. She sat up and wrapped herself in his arms. They clung to each other awkwardly until he let her back gently and lay down beside her. Neither said a word for a long, long time.

"Polly was over here this afternoon."

He dreaded what would follow. "How is she?"

"She's going back to Suffield."

He didn't answer.

The room held no conversation that night. The lights remained off. Ellie went into the bathroom to remove her clothes. Howard was in his pajamas when she returned. He looked at her. Beautiful, lissome—as he had once referred to her—blossoming with child. She was a creature to be kept close. She was his wife, an adored possession.

That next day, Ken popped into his BOQ room to say goodbye.

"Where you going?" Howard was aghast.

"The Ol' Man wants me up at Regimental Headquarters. Something in S-3. Gawd knows, but who cares? Gets me out of the trenches."

"Christ, everybody's leaving! What about Chew?"

"Oh, they'll get another Platoon Leader, and Chew can take him on."

And that's the way it worked. Men moved in and out changing jobs, stripes were divvied out, men becoming P.F.C.s., Corporals, Buck Sergeants, Squad Leaders, Assistants. Things moved fast. An air of impending catastrophe cut in and out of extended boredom. Weeks raced by. The phrase "hurry-up-and-wait" became a watchword.

In June, Camp Meade became a madhouse. Howard was ordered to report to the 3rd Battalion Commanding Officer, Major Clifton Harris. Like many officers, Major Harris had been given the responsibility of Battalion C. O. but not the rank. Loud, with the bite of a bulldog, Harris kept the 3d Battalion hopping, obviously coveting the day when the gold leaf on his collar would turn to silver.

"Andrews? I'm relieving you from your platoon and making you Battalion Radio Officer. Your Headquarters Company Commanding Officer will be Captain Whalen. Report in to him when we're through here."

Howard's baffled expression obviously fueled the Major's irritation, but he rolled right through it. "You certainly know more than anyone else in this battalion after that antenna you put up. You've got a good background, speak a little French, I understand . . . do you?"

"Yes, Sir. Some."

" . . . and your Battery Commander, Captain Lewis, says you're a good officer." He paused a bit and added undiplomatically, "Fact is, I don't have much choice. I need somebody, and you're it."

A staff job, he thought. That's a step up, no matter how it was phrased. Howard was pleased as punch.

"Word is that we'd better get all the training we can as quickly as we can, because the 351st is leaving the Brigade and joining the 'Buffalo' Division in France. We'll be 'on the line' by the end of the year. Now, there's more to this, so head on over to Regimental Headquarters and report to Colonel Eckhart. He's got another assignment for you."

Howard saluted, spun about and double-timed to the 351st. The sergeant told him to "go right on in."

Colonel. Eckhart was marching up and down before two obviously frightened lieutenants. " . . . and you'll find out what the hell's going on over there and make whatever preparations you think necessary to get your battalions up and running with whatever-the-hell communication system those Frogs are using. God knows they're not telling us a damn thing."

Howard slipped in beside the other two officers without a sound. Colonel Eckhart stared at him a second. "You're Third Battalion Radio Officer?"

"Lieutenant Andrews, Sir."

"Good." The Colonel shook his hand and nodded to the others. "This here's Lieutenants Plumb and Newton, First and Second Battalion Radio Officers." Then he shouted over his shoulder in a burst that all but shook the walls. "Sergeant, tell Hall to get in here."

"Howdy do, howdy do, howdy do," the muffled greetings went around the trio. Newton, a cadaver-like, gray-faced kid, looked like he'd crawled out from under a rock. Plumb was like the rock itself, short and about forty-five pounds overweight. *Must be awfully good at what they do,* Howard thought.

"You called, Sir?"

Howard spun around at the familiar voice. "Ken!" he blurted out.

"You two know each other?" broke in Colonel.Eckhart.

"Yes, Sir, we went to school together and then Plattsburg, and a couple of weeks ago we were in the same Battalion," Ken said smiling. "Good to see you, Howey."

Howard's eyes were riveted on the silver bar pinned to Ken's collar. He felt the blood drain from his face.

"Yeah," Ken whispered. "Got a promotion."

"First Lieutenant!" Howard almost choked on the words. He tried not to sound anything but pleased.

"Hell, Howey, 'rank among Lieutenants is like virtue among whores'," Ken said, beaming. Newton grinned, but Plumb laughed outright.

The Colonel left little time for chit-chat. "Hall is Assistant Regimental S-3, Operations. The four of you are going over early to set up our training program in France. We have no idea how we're to communicate with the Division or the spotters or anybody in that Godforsaken country, for that matter. Get your gear in shape to leave on call."

By the time she was on a train back to Springfield, Ellie was huge. Buddy was due in two months, they felt sure. The greatcoat flowed about her like a Confederate belle's hoop. No one commented on it, but Buddy was considerable in size. In the haze of departing they forgot all about her misery at the Stewarts'.

"I did so want to be here when you sail."

"And I wanted to be here when Buddy arrives. But I can't let you sit in a room in Baltimore with only Mrs. Stewart and her old maid daughters to help. You're spunky, you're my Blessed, but now you need your own people around you all the time."

"I'll miss you. Promise me you won't drink."

Howard grinned. "You know the only reason Pa drinks is because he had two girls."

"Howard, you're terrible. Please, promise."

"I promise."

They went on and on, showering each other with aches and concerns till the whistle blew and Howard scrambled for the door. He watched the parlor car move slowly out of the Baltimore station. In his hand were three sealed envelopes, one labeled, "To be opened the day you sail," another, "To be opened the day you arrive" and on the third was written the words, "To be read the day you receive the Buddy cable." Fate allowed him to read the first in less than a week:

> *Blessedest,*
>
> *I don't know how I'm going to act, or rather (by the time you read this) how I have acted, but if I haven't been every bit as spunky as I should be, I hope you hair-brushed me properly . . . I'm a selfish little beast not to want to lend you even long enough to straighten out this war muddle . . . . Never in my life have I been so proud of anything as I am that I have a husband who has seen his duty and gone straight ahead to do it.*

. . . there are so many, many ways yet, in which I must change if I ever expect to be the kind of wife and mother you want me to be, and I know too, that you're not going to be standing still. You can't face the big issues you must face, without growing bigger yourself.

. . . Dearest, it's going to be heavenly to have each other again, all the more because we've suffered.

I'll pray for you every night, dear, and I want you to do the same for me—and Buddy. For months now I've been able to formulate just one prayer, "God keep my boy and make me worthy of him."

Ellie

Chapter Ten

Howard leaned his weight against the three-eighths-inch-thick steel plate that topped the prow of the *Leviathan*. Early morning Adirondacks air drifted down the Hudson from Bear Mountain, moist and clean smelling. Its mist hung over the water separating the *Leviathan* in New Jersey from Hell's Kitchen on the lower West Side of New York, turning downtown Manhattan into an impressionist watercolor wash.

As C.L.I. had stripped him from Manhattan's dismal West Side, as the New York Sun had thrust him into respectability, as a set of gold bars had elevated him to "Gentleman By Act of Congress," this war would redefine Howard G. Andrews.

Howard wore eagerness like a cloak. He wanted to push the giant vessel from its Hoboken slip, head it down the bay and through the Narrows eastward into the open sea. "Over There," as Cohan penned it, to France, to the "Zone of the Advance," the front line of the American Expeditionary Force. Only the laws of physics kept him from moving the ship by himself.

"Whatcha' lookin' at, Howey?"

It took conscious effort to turn around and face the voice. "What . . . . "

Ken Hall stood framed by the *Leviathan's* massive superstructure. It was the greatest seagoing vessel in the world. The ship's broad bow was completely empty except for the two of them. Howard, the kid from Hell's Kitchen, the orphan dumped on CLI's doorstep and, now, the lowly Second Lieutenant facing his superior officer, First Lieutenant Kenneth Hall of the Suffield's illustrious Halls. He struggled to force the true world into focus.

Ken was smiling. "Taking a last look at the old home town?"

"I was thinking about where we were going, what we're going to do . . . . "

"And what we're leaving behind," Ken added, looking up river. "I know."

"No, you don't," Howard responded as he turned back to the open water.

"What's that supposed to mean?"

It took a moment for Howard to finish bringing his thoughts together. "I didn't mean anything." He pivoted slowly to Ken. "I was just thinking that life gives us some funny . . . options . . . doesn't it?" He tried to smile back.

"If you mean whether we get shot or just blown away, I guess you're right."

"Well," Howard sighed, nodding as he turned again to the Hudson, "sometimes it gives us a chance to do the blowing away ourselves." He was too absorbed in his own thoughts to realize the length of time it took Ken to answer. The voice had turned icy.

"Plumb and The Newt are watching the Ohio National Guard coming onto the dock." There were a few moments before he continued in a flat, noncommittal way, "Why don't you come watch them board?"

Howard didn't respond. More silence passed before he heard Ken's hard rubber heels receding on the metal deck. When he finally turned, Ken had reached the other officers amidships, staring down onto the Hoboken dock. Plumb waved a chubby arm to come join them.

"Hey, Howey!" he shouted. "You gotta see this. Hurry! They're coming on board right now."

"Who?" Howard called back.

"The whole Ohio National Guard, thousands of them."

Howard headed aft along the starboard side. Lieutenant Bill Newton was elbow-draped over the gunnel, angular and diffident. The trio had long since dubbed him The Newt. A perfect pseudonym. Lieutenant Plumb's first name, it turned out, was Rollo, so, round as he was, he'd become The Rolling Plum.

Below, canvassed walkways fed the great ship. Men yoked with duffle-bags linked at the draw string staggered along the gangways in the hazy early morning light. *Cannon fodder*, he thought. *War's nutrition.*

"Look over there." Ken pointed to a small knot of officers in the morning shadows. "Two stars!" Ken hissed. The Commanding Officer was there, indeed, surrounded by more Bird Colonels and top-flight brass than Howard had seen clumped together at one time in his military career, together with officers from Canada and even France and England.

The Rolling Plum called from the sliding doorway behind them, "Come on! Follow me. Want to show you something."

The four raced up three levels to "A" deck where Plumb pulled them into a clump with a "Shush" and a finger to his lips. Howard rasped, "What are we doing up here? This deck is off limits."

"Not as long as it's empty."

They laughed as Plumb headed down the narrow, carpeted hall, its polished handrails studded with shining brass fixtures. Howard looked to Ken, but all he got was a shrug and a "Why not?" What the hell, he thought, Ken has the rank. Let him take the responsibility. The three scrambled after, like high school kids off to tilt outhouses.

Past huge staterooms with creamy white carpets, overstuffed sofas and enameled coffee tables topped with samovars and bone china, past porcelain shower stalls with gold plated faucets, past chapels, dispensaries, hospital wards, down, down into the bowels of the ship and a dining hall the size of two tennis courts.

A soft, rumbling sound caused the four to turn. "You gentlemen have a reason for being here?"

A fully decorated Captain in the U.S. Navy loomed over the khaki quartet, one eyebrow raised quizzically, an almost imperceptible smile beneath a forest of facial hair.

Howard was the closest. The best he could do was a mumble: "No, sir."

"I believe you gentlemen are restricted to "B" Deck. When the time comes you'll hear the bell for mess call quite clearly from there." His gentle nod dismissed the assemblage with the quick, clean sweep of a broom. They moved like lint in the drift through the carpeted hallways, Howard to the rear, his face black with embarrassment and rage.

"Damn fool, stupid, idiotic thing!"

"What the hell's the matter with you, Howey," Ken called as he ran.

"You! You stupid idiot!"

Ken spun to a stop amidst the stairwell. "Watch yourself, Howey. You're no wizard, yourself."

"At least I'm smart enough to know what's off-limits and what's not."

"Watch your mouth . . . . Lieutenant!" There was a long and searing pause before that word, "Lieutenant!" And Howey knew what was going on in Ken's mind during that pause. The others appeared to as well, because The Rolling Plumb broke the silence . . . and the tension . . . with the old Army aphorism, "Rank among Lieutenants is like virtue among whores." Howey froze.

Ken took a moment and then turned to Plumb with a grin. "Race you to the deck," he called and darted up the stairs, The Rolling Plumb puffing in his wake. At the starboard rail they hunched together, lighting cigarettes, Howard still gnawing at his bitterness.

Several minutes passed before Plumb again spoke.

"Sure is a big boat."

"It's a ship, dumkopf," The Newt snapped.

"Oh." A pause. "You know what this 'ship' was?" burbled Plumb. "*The Fatherland*! Property of the North German Lloyd line."

"'*Der Vaterland*'!" echoed The Newt.

"It was docked here in Hoboken," Plumb went on, "and when we joined the Allies the Germans jammed up its engines, blew holes in the hull and just about sunk her, right here in the Hudson."

"They locked up the Germans as POWs," Bill Newton interjected, "changed its name from *'Der Vaterland'* to *'The Leviathan'*, and the Navy took over. When they finished putting things back together, it went two knots faster than before!"

Below, the endless, pendulous wave of khakied humanity, like rations being fed the *Leviathan* maw, was hypnotic. The ship was the war itself, gorging on America's finest, four open mouths, two to a deck, a giant deformed suckling with never ending resources. Give us your tired, your worn, your yearning to be heroes! Glory ahead!

The irony of traveling luxury-class to death in the trenches was penetrating. Howard allowed himself a hidden smile and wondered if there wasn't a touch of insanity in the air, if the world wasn't taunting him with an idiotic grin and the soft cooing of fools, "You want? You want?"

Edging through the silence, the murmured shuffling below no more than a distant burble of sound, slowly the words and melody, " . . . what's the use of worrying . . . " snaked into his consciousness. " . . . it never was worth while . . . "

Howard turned to see . . . and hear . . . The Newt softly singing:

Pack up your troubles in your ol' kit bag and
Smile, smile, smile.
While you've a 'lucifer' to light your 'fag'
Smile, boys, that's the style.
What's the use of worrying,
It never was worth while, so . . .
Pack up your troubles in your old kit bag and
Smile, smile, smile!"

Hours later, the four members of the 351st advance team were sitting in the salon, linen napkins laid neatly across laps, when the sound . . . the feel . . . of giant engines vibrated throughout the ship. It was an odd, resonating sensation, something akin to Howey's first experience being astride a horse back in Plattsburg. But this was a monstrous, metallic beast that lifted their iron world in majestic slow motion. Officers, hundreds of them, stared at each other as the perception communicated itself around the salon. "We're heading out!"

First one, then a dozen and then hoards slipped from their chairs and raced mutely to the outer decks to catch a glimpse of the New Jersey skyline slipping off to the rear, bands playing a military romance on the Hoboken docks. The sailing was about as secret as a Fourth of July parade with hundreds of crafts of all sizes racing about the Upper Bay, a mad cacophony of sirens screaming, horns blaring, bells clanging.

Ahead, Manhattan slowly pivoted and positioned itself Portside. At the waterline, half-a-dozen tugs nudged the giant hull back and forth until, straight ahead, the Statue of Liberty lifted her arm to show the way. The ship listed slightly as thousands raced Starboard to view the Green Goddess, their eyes wet with salt tears, of course the fault of Atlantic spray.

Soon the ship was through The Narrows, tugs dropping away, one still standing by for the Harbor Pilot set to turn the helm over to the U. S. Navy's Captain. There was a slight shudder as the screws reversed and the ship came to a standstill. A gangway reached down to let the Pilot descend, turn to throw the Captain a salute and then step aboard the ship's last contact with the United States.

Not quite, however, for out of nowhere appeared a bevy of destroyers cutting across the bow like mustangs, ringing about in a mathematical display of high-speed maneuvering, dipping their colors in a final salute before speeding back to port.

Scuttlebutt informed all landlubbers that the *Leviathan* would greet the open sea alone. No convoy could keep up with her. Four 8-inch guns mounted fore and aft were protection enough—that and its incredible speed and, of course, a lot of zig-zagging. Word spread through the ship that the Germans knew to the minute when they had left Hoboken and were, as usual, lying in wait for their "Vaterland." But with the word also came assurances that no one, not even the Kaiser's indefatigable Unterseebooten could catch the now-christened *Leviathan.*

Howard was assigned to the corridors, keeping the Ohio National Guard in line as the men marched by company to the enlisted men's mess hall, picked up their trays and stood around chest-high tables gorging food. More than ten thousand soldiers quickly turned one of the world's great luxury liners into a sweaty, brine-and-urine-smelling sinkhole.

Watching them move like moles, sullen, overseas caps pushed back from sweaty foreheads, Howard smiled at his own foresight. Maybe he was just a lowly shavetail, but he had a full-sized bed with crisp white linens and a white-tiled bathroom with porcelain shower. R. H. I. P.—"Rank Has Its Privileges!"

Officers Call at seventeen hundred hours brought announcements, questions and answers, followed by rumors and complaints. All matches had to be turned in.

"Use the propane lighters along the inner corridors to light your 'fags'. 'Lucifers' attract subs," the Commander barked. "So does trash overboard. Even a match stick. Turn 'em in!" They did. Except for the few squirreled away. "At sunset, everyone inside. At twenty-hundred, lights out all over the ship."

In a few days, the routine became routine. But no one could keep up with the time. Every hour or so the clock would jump ahead. "Chow time?" "Lights out already?" "Hell, I just got to sleep!"

"Every man in a life jacket!" boomed the ship's loud speaker. Officers on the fo'c'sle glanced quickly about, some pulling the cork vests from where they served to soften seating on the harsh metal deck. Arms and elbows squirmed through canvas straps for a few frantic moments, and, as suddenly as it had started, the ballet ceased and boredom regained its hold. A card was dealt, a page was turned and backs again lined the rail.

"Boat Drill! Abandon Ship!!" The voice had the urgency of Armageddon, but bodies moving toward lifeboats, now grown dull through repetition, treated the process with disdain. The *Leviathan* would never sink, the Germans would never find them, the U. S. Army was invincible!

"No trash overboard! No trash overboard! U-Boats in the area. No trash overboard!!"

"Hell," the Newt whined, "they talk about making the world safe for Democracy, and you can't even spit in the ocean."

Howard reached into his footlocker. Balancing the writing desk on one palm, he slowly unwrapped the protective towel.

"What's that?"

Howard hadn't noticed Ken watching him. Lugging a fancy wedding gift into the war zone wasn't easy to justify. "It's a writing desk," he answered hesitantly.

Ken nodded. "Looks nice. That's what you used to work with on the 'Sun'?"

Howard couldn't tell if he was joshing him. "No. Ellie gave it to me."

"Really?" Ken seemed interested. "Let me see it."

Howard removed the towel and held the box out. The brass hinges and latch, the inlaid wood brightly polished, were all strangely out of place, even on a luxury liner. But Ken was obviously impressed.

"Can you open it?"

"Sure." Howard snapped the catch and opened it to the felt covered panel. He pulled up the tab revealing the pen and ink holder. But he stopped there. The other sections were private, the places where he stored his notes, plus sheets and sheets of blank, white paper, just waiting, waiting—and his little picture of Ellie.

"That . . . is really neat," Ken acknowledged, taking the box from him. He peeked into it, turning it, closed the desk, rotated the latch and, with a respectful nod, handed it back to Howard. "That is really neat."

It was clear that only New England reticence prohibited Ken from asking more. Howard decided to leave it that way.

Topside, Howard wedged himself into the angle of steel where airvent met deck, the bulky cork vest now second nature with every comfort-seeking effort. He looked around first and then cracked open his inlaid treasure, balancing the fully extended writing desk on his fully extended legs. After another surreptitious glance he popped open the pen and ink compartment and extracted the miniature picture of Ellie. It was only an inch or so square, but her bright eyes and slight smile, even in miniature, brought her closer. On the back were the simple words, "I do," written on their brief honeymoon in Rockport. A reminder of a cherished commitment.

After yet another quick glance around, he pulled a sheet of fresh paper from inside the lid, balanced the writing desk, then unscrewed the tin cap on the tiny ink bottle, dipped the straight pen and made the first mark in his War To End All Wars saga. "Mother Carey's Chickens," he wrote across the top.

> *Stormy Petrels, great omens of good luck, wave their wings as they swoop over the deck of the giant ship Leviathan and turn homeward for the land the doughboys left behind. Navy Jacks call them 'Mother Carey's Chickens,' and they are the last vestige of home America's fighting men see as the troop ship plows majestically eastward . . . .*

"Hey, Howey, whatcha' doing?" The Rolling Plum loomed over Howard like a barn door.

"I'm writing an article."

"For the 'Sun'?"

"Maybe. Maybe the 'Post'."

"Hey, that's neat. Didya' see the porpoises?"

"No. Where?"

"There's a hundred of them dancing all around the right side of the bow."

"Are they feeding them?"

"You kidding? Anybody throws anything overboard on this ship's finishing the ride in the brig." Then he was gone.

Howard scratched out the title and wrote over it, "Sea Birds and Mammals" and penned his next line:

> *. . . while below a huge school of porpoises played leapfrog in the water below."*

He scratched through "*school*" and wrote "*pod*" but then stared at it a moment, wondering which was right. He watched Plumb and the other officers laughing like school children at the ship-side antics and then the French and English officers playing make-shift golf with swagger sticks and wads of paper for golf balls.

CHAPTER ELEVEN

"Gentlemen, settle down! Quiet, please. Quiet! Get settled quickly." The Navy Commander was shouting over the din of uniformed "brass" shuffling into the salon for Officers Call. "Settle down! Settle down quickly."

Off to one side, the grizzly-faced Captain of the ship who had confronted the 351st advance team in the mess hall stood patiently, hands locked behind his back. It was his first public appearance in their four days at sea, and though few but Howard, Ken Hall, the Newt and the Rolling Plum knew who he was, the gold stripes set tongues wagging. In seconds the salon was quiet as a tomb.

"Gentlemen, the Ship's Captain has a word for you."

There was a brief rustle as the Commander stepped aside and the Captain moved down center on the little band platform apparently left, conveniently, from Lloyd Line days. The Captain's rumbling voice came through the crowded hall as clearly as it had just inches from Howard's face.

"Gentlemen, I know you have been informed that the voyage would take but five days. Well . . . it will not."

The Captain didn't get to be Captain without knowing how to play the role, and the pause covered the length of time necessary for muffled response and instant suppression.

"We have received word that our *Boche* friends have sent us an escort, two *unterseabooten* to be precise, and they lie directly in our path. They know, of course, that they cannot surface without being seen and they cannot pursue us because they haven't the speed above water any more than they have below. All they can do is lie and wait for us and then launch a torpedo."

Once again, a rumble throughout the salon. This time, senior officers glared down the response. The Captain's timing was superb.

"Now, it is not our intention to be courted, however attractive the confrontation might turn out to be." A slight chuckle seeped through the whiskers inviting a similar response. "What we plan," he continued, "is a bit of zig-zagging which will add a few days to our journey." *Buzzing throughout the salon.* "I won't tell you where we'll zig and where we'll zag," *slight buzz mixed with laughter* "but if you should spy the chalky coastline of Britain, fear not that we are diverting you from the enjoyable task of thrashing the Kaiser." *Greater laughter.* "Rest assured. You will debark in France. Our Port of Entry will be the city of Brest."

Like an actor on cue, the Captain nodded to the elite, turned on his heels and departed amidst thunderous applause. Why the officers applauded wasn't quite clear to Howard. But the two-star general of the Ohio National Guard was on the podium in seconds instructing his contingent how to inform the men, deal with questions and assure everyone as to the safety of the ship. However, he emphasized, the trip was now going to take a week—not five days.

Morning of the seventh day found the 351st advanced quartet in the forward corridors of "B" deck. All through the previous night Howard had felt the shudder and heave accompanying each zig and zag. As the sun lifted over the water he saw England's chalk cliffs off to the left front. Abruptly, the *Leviathan* wheeled hard to starboard, and there, far across the Channel, was a strip of land jutting westward into the sea, land that would be their new home.

Then, with startling surprise, a flurry of destroyers appeared from behind on the starboard side and dashed across the *Leviathan*'s bow in repetition of the send-off outside New York Harbor. Like bees, the tiny ships darted over to every piece of floating scrap that might look like a periscope as the *Leviathan* knifed its way to the looming coastline of France.

Howard moved away from the rest of his quartet, leaned against the gunnel and removed Ellie's two remaining letters from his breast pocket. He returned the Buddy letter to his pocket, but before opening the one labeled "When you arrive," he penciled on the envelope: "Sunday, June 23rd, 1918—Brest, France."

Honeykins:

Are you really there? . . . There are so many things I wish I knew. I wonder where you are landing, France, Italy or England . . . I hope everything went well, dear. Somehow seasickness would be a little "out of uniform" for a good looking lieutenant, to say nothing of being mighty inconvenient and uncomfortable.

. . . Wouldn't it be strange if you should find the Buddy Message there waiting for you? . . . Blessed, isn't it funny to write about something we know nothing about?

Oh, Dearheart, how I do love you. It's the dearest thing in my life.

Ellie

Howard thought of the packet of letters he had written Ellie, letters waiting to be turned in for the ship's return voyage. The seven days at sea had produced not quite the one-a-day he'd promised, but at least he'd doubled up a couple of times to bring the pack to half-a-dozen. He tried to imagine how long it would take his letters to Ellie to reach America, go by train to Springfield and then be delivered to 345 Riverdale Street. It was good he'd put all those sugary things in them after all. But, funny, until he looked at the "Buddy" letter envelope, he hadn't thought much about Buddy. Oh well, there was a war going on. And besides, he'd cranked out three good articles for the *New York Sun.*

An hour later, they were anchored in the harbor at Brest, and cumbersome lighters were ferrying the men to shore. Footlockers and bedrolls were stacked along the deck, and Howard's letters destined for stateside had been deposited in one of the slotted boxes posted every few hundred yards. He and the Newt hunched over the rail watching Ohio's National Guard evacuate the ship.

"Betcha we were damn near England," the Newt mumbled. Howard thought of Tommy Ross and wondered if he was flying yet. And wouldn't it be great if Tommy had been up over the Channel that very morning and seen the *Leviathan* streaking in and then wheeling south to the continent. He would have to ask Tommy. It didn't occur to him that he and Tommy were just two men out of a million, that the chance of connecting was as remote as that of the *unterseabooten Kapitan* linking up with the *Leviathan.*

The Newt pointed a long finger past Howard's nose. "Look over there," he commanded. "There's a sub with a white flag on it."

"You mean at the docks? God, Newt, that's two miles away. You can't see that."

"No it's not, and yes I can."

Ken joined them from midships where he and Plumb had been watching bleary-eyed men file down the lone gangway into the "lighters."

"Hey, fellahs, there's a sub tied up in there."

"Told ya," interjected the Newt.

Plumb rolled in behind Ken. "The guys on one of the lighters say the sub was one trying to catch us."

He repeated scuttlebutt that *Herr Kapitan* had pulled into Brest with a half-starved, stir-crazed crew, choosing to surrender rather than stay out as ordered till they sank their stolen *Vaterland.* They'd missed her on two trips before, and they were out of food, water and fuel.

"I guess it was healthier to surrender to the A.E.F. than to return to the Kaiser empty handed. Wonder what happened to the other sub."

"Look at the tiny trains," interrupted the Newt.

Waiting along a web of tracks were wooden box cars, a dozen or more strung out behind each steaming locomotive.

"'Forty-Or-Eight'," submitted Ken.

"'Forty-Or-Eight' what?" queried the Rolling Plum.

"Forty men or eight horses. That's what those box cars hold."

There was a slight pause. Howard asked, straight-faced, "Which are we?"

Ken gave him a side glance but said nothing. The Rolling Plum guffawed.

Officers debarked last—military etiquette—with bedrolls and footlockers seen to by men in the ranks. Field Grade officers, majors and up, had the luxury of first-class coaches, four compartments with beautifully upholstered seating. Second class wasn't quite so luxurious. Third class seated ten or twelve on plain, wooden benches. Last, of course, were the "forty-or-eight." In this case, that meant forty buck privates in the Ohio National Guard. The entire Guard then rolled out onto the French countryside.

The 351st Advanced Party debarked last, along with the Canadian, French and English officers. Their lighter came to rest just yards from the German sub, the pitiful white sheet still dangling from its periscope. Howard wondered what it would be like captured by the Germans, but he kept his silence.

"English Spoken" signs were everywhere. As many soldiers, jackies and marines filled the streets of Brest as there were natives, and the A.E.F. was welcomed effusively.

"Bless you," he cried. "Oh, bless you, Messieurs les Americains! Bless you."

Hobbling on a cane, the old graybeard looked like a veteran of the War of 1870. He patted the four uniforms, tears in his eyes, and then reached for Bill Newton's hands with both of his own. Leering up with a toothless grin he whined:

"Geev me cigarette!"

The romance of France disappeared right along with the cadged cigarette. Oh, well. They were here to save the world.

Surprise! The American Expeditionary Forces H.Q. in Brest was located over a garage! At the top of the back stairs a major sat behind an ancient table shuffling papers and writing in a large ledger. He gave them an exasperated look.

"Who's in charge?"

Ken acknowledged the responsibility.

"You go see the Colonel over there, and the rest of you sign in here and then wait downstairs."

"How long's it going to be?" asked the Rolling Plum.

The major looked at him a moment before answering. "Probably most of the afternoon."

"What about mail?"

Howard's question provoked a quizzical frown.

"You mean sending or getting?"

"Well, I meant mail from the States."

"Lieutenant, you're not even attached to a unit. How is anyone supposed to write you here?"

"They gave us a provisional unit and an APO address," Howard answered lamely. He handed the major a copy of their orders.

The major looked at the paper and sighed. "There's an APO at the Y.M.C.A. Check with them," he grumbled, handing the paper back, "but I doubt you'll be here long enough to get anything from the States. And while you're at the "Y", you might as well ask them about quarters. That's where most of the officers stay."

"You fellahs go on," suggested Ken. "Get a place for us, and meet me here around five."

"Take a streetcar to the modern part of town," the major added. "Someone there can direct you to the 'Y'. Any of you speak French?"

"I do," Howard answered. The others looked at him, surprised. "A little," he added.

The four of them signed in and then went back downstairs and outside the garage.

"You didn't tell me you spoke French," said the Newt.

"Well, we studied it at C.L.I. I can say, '*Ouvrez la fenetre and jettez vous*'." Howard gave him a grin.

The Newt frowned suspiciously. "What does that mean?"

"It means 'open the window and jump out'."

The Rolling Plum laughed. The Newt glowered.

Chapter Twelve

A toy-like conveyance clanged by, loaded to the roof. The American trio climbed aboard. Old men, old women, young women with bad teeth all stared and smiled apologetically.

"*Ou est le Y.M.C.A. Americain?*" Howard asked, measuring his phrases.

The trolley driver was a post-middle-aged lady with a rag coat and spiked heels. She eyed Howard narrowly and answered quickly, "*Regardez moi, et-ecoutez.*"

"*Merci,*" Howard answered.

As the trolley lumbered forward, Plumb expressed his respect. "Hey, you're not bad."

After some fifteen minutes of bell clanging, crawling, racing, and veering side to side through narrow thoroughfares, the spike-heeled woman called out, "Allez vous, maintenent" and, barely stopping the ancient contraption, let the trio off in front of the Y.M.C.A.

Inside, courtesy lessened. It was an American, a civilian this time, but a tired and harried one. "Sorry, full up. Try a hotel."

"Wait a minute," the Newt cut in. "Where's the APO here?"

"Over in the corner," was the answer.

The so-called Army Post Office turned out to be several antique tables with makeshift shelves labeled for different units, one large suspended canvas bag for "everything else" and a lone corporal busy rummaging through sacks of incoming mail.

Plumb stuck his orders under the enlisted man's nose and asked, "Any incoming mail for us?"

The trio received a haggard look and a slow, somewhat incredulous shake of the head as the corporal scanned the orders. "Sir, didn't you just arrive here?" The question was rhetorical and the respect minimal.

Howard interrupted. "I'd like to send a cable."

The corporal's mouth dropped. "A what?"

"A cable. To my wife."

The corporal turned and called, "Lieutenant?" Then he explained, "He's the Censor."

From a far corner, a fresh-faced second lieutenant scurried over. "Cables are only for emergencies," he pointed out.

"But my wife is very sick," Howard whispered dramatically. "And she's expecting a baby. If she doesn't hear that I arrived safely she may lose the baby . . . and she may not live!"

Plumb and the Newt stepped back slightly as the Censor appeared to seek verification from them. "OK, but put the address and the message on this," he finally agreed and handed Howard a rumpled pad of forms.

As he wrote, Howard furthered his gamble: "What if the baby comes and she's all right? Can she cable me back?"

The Censor leaned close. "When's the baby due?"

"In another week or so."

"Look, her cable's going to go to London. They'll then send it by regular mail to your unit, wherever you are. That'll take about as long as it does for a stateside letter. If I wire my buddy in London to be on a lookout for something addressed to you, he can forward it to me as a wire, and I'll forward the wire to the French cable office in the town where you're quartered. That way you'll get it in a couple of days." He leaned back with a conspiratorial grin and nodded as if to say, "How's that!"

Howard shook hands with the young lieutenant and paid the cable fee, grinning like a Cheshire Cat.

Outside, both Plumb and Newton's admiration escalated.

"Hell, that's nothing," Howard protested. "That's the way we do things in New York. Ya' gotta' have a little Moxie."

Hotels in Brest registered *Les Americains* with a vengeance.

"Name? Age? Nationality? Color?" One had no secrets in France. "Condition of servitude?" What was that? Oh, rank! *Lieutenant.* "Disposition?" I guess that means *The War.* "Expected length of stay?" Ha! That one's funny.

"Thees way, pleeeze."

Up the narrow stairway to the suite, bedroom parlor, bath, balcony overlooking the street, grand piano and risque pictures on the wall. But the sign on the door read, "Priz: 30 francs."

Ten francs each! That was $1.80! That plus 15 francs per person, per day for meals would run $4.50. Le Directeur was informed that the limit was 6 francs per day! They got their rooms, at 6 francs per lieutenant per day. And so it went.

At dusk, Ken Hall joined them in the tiny but rather quaint hotel. His report came as a mixed blessing.

"Here's the big picture. Nobody here knows what the hell's going on. How about that? So we're here for at least a week with me tied to a chair over the garage and you fellahs free to sight-see."

"I thought we were here because we were Battalion Radio Officers," Howard grumbled.

"Come on, Howey, the Colonel really did want a leg up on communications. But I can tell you honestly that nobody here has the vaguest idea what A.E.F. Headquarters has in mind for the 351st."

"Then why are we here so early?"

Ken glowered. "Howey, simmer down. We're in one of the nicest towns in France. Take a hike around. There's no reason you can't enjoy yourselves." He eyed him closely. "Buy Ellie some lace. And get something for your baby. It's about due, isn't it?"

Remembering Ken's comment about children, Howard searched for a sign of confirmation or criticism, but there was neither.

That next morning, Howard awakened to the sight and sound of the Rolling Plum peering into his room.

"Got an extra Gem Blade?"

"Gawd Almighty, Plumb, can't you knock?"

"Did knock." The door swung wide as the undershirted body projected itself toward the wash stand.

Howard pulled the covers against the cold morning and Plumb's fiddling with his toilet case. He popped up in time to see the rotund form heading back to the door waving a tiny, paper-wrapped Gem razor blade as he went.

"You had five. Won't miss this one," he announced and swung the door shut after himself.

Howard cursed, thrashing about in the blankets and sheets. Time intervened.

Knock, Knock!

"Heading back to Headquarters, Howey. You fellahs take it easy."

"Jesus! Can't a guy sleep?"

There was a slight pause. Then the voice—now distinctly Ken Hall's—answered a bit slower and more deliberately, "Behave yourself, Lieutenant. See you around five."

Eyes wide open, Howard waited until the footsteps had receded. Quietly he muttered, "Gawd. Jesus. Damn fools."

Knock, knock!

"Oh, Christ," he moaned.

It seemed minutes before a second set of knocks sounded.

"Howey, are you in there?"

He recognized the Newt this time. "What the hell do you want?"

There was a pause before Bill Newton answered through the closed door. "For the sake of the girl you left behind, I hope this isn't the way you wake up every morning."

Again, footsteps faded. This time Howard lay still, the Newt's words echoing.

The scene in Plattsburg when he had to apologize for being such a grouch and another in Baltimore when Ellie had cried, these and others played in his mind. He'd been terrified that "surliness," his "bearishness" as he called it, would make her detest him. But he truly believed that his grouches were a thing of the past, that marriage had produced a real understanding. It was her cheerfulness, her joy in the simplest things, her smile when they met, those first words each morning, those cheerful words that lasted all day, these things had changed him. He truly believed.

Chapter Thirteen

There is something eternally right about an old New England family tree, Howard mused. The symmetry, the presence of all its branches. One branch isn't just dropped off without warning, before its time, or be sent off to be fed by other trees or just lie cut off and discarded on the ground. Each branch is a . . .

Pa's a drunk! Maude's voice cut through his memory.

Yes, but he didn't throw you out. He didn't toss one branch here and another one there. Besides, Pa is a respected member of society, a State Game Warden, the owner of a huge farm, a real estate man, an entrepreneur who brought automobiles into . . .

He went bankrupt. Maude's voice interrupted again. *Made us sell the farm, the house, move to Springfield.*

Howard's brain whirled on the imaginary Maude and lashed angrily at the rebellious voice. *Your father is a saint compared to mine. Mine sent my sister to the in-laws and gave . . . me . . . away!*

"Howey, what the hell are you mumbling about?"

Howard looked up from his plate and stared blankly at The Newt.

"Are you gonna eat that lobster or are you just gonna wait. till it crawls off the plate and hoists itself up your tie and into your mouth?"

The Rolling Plumb giggled. "This is the biggest Goddamned lobster I've ever seen. I'm not sure it wouldn't bite Howey's head off if it ever got up off that plate."

The Newt glowered at him. "I think he's day dreaming about the honey-pie he left back home." "Don't forget, he's gonna be a daddy soon," Plumb added. "When this war's over he's gonna have to buy lotsa' lobsters. I bet he's gonna have a dozen kids."

"More," added The Newt. "Pretty boy with the moustache is gonna keep that girl running from room to room."

"All right, now, that's enough," Howard ordered.

"Oooh, testy," giggled Plumb.

"I'll test both of you guys with the back of my hand." Howard pushed his way from the table and headed out of the restaurant. On the veranda he stood looking over the harbor thinking about Tommy and his airplanes somewhere in. the English countryside. But his mind drifted back to the scene of Tommy as his Best Man at the wedding, with Ellie in flowing white stepping down from the porch on Riverdale Street and gliding across the lawn to take her place at his side. The preacher intoned, *"Do you take Eleanor Arlington to be your . . . "*

Howard answered aloud. "I take her, and I take her Ma and Pa and sister Maude, and I promise to hold on to them and keep my family together, for ever and ever, Amen."

Plumb and The Newt were coming out of the restaurant. "Hey, you owe us for part of that lobster."

Howard turned and stared blankly at the two.

"What's the matter with you, Howey?"

"You guys don't have any idea what the responsibility of a wife and family means, do you?" he asked evenly.

"Just more people who'll boss you around," said Plumb with a degree of uncertainty.

"No," said The Newt, "it's people you're in charge of. People you're responsible for feeding and housing and clothing. I know what you're thinking and what you're going through, Howey, and I know it must be tough being over here, so far from your wife when she's having your first kid. A family is a lot of responsibility."

Howard remained silent. Finally, Plumb grinned and added, "At least it won't be a whole platoon."

"That's Command Responsibility," answered The Newt. "A family is different." Howard's head whipped around, and he stared at The Newt. "How?"

"Well, a family is a lot of give and take . . . "

"So's a platoon," Howard snapped.

"That's not what I mean," The Newt fumbled. "With a platoon you've got the final word. The bar on your shoulder backs you up, and no matter what you want or say you want that little gold bar backs you up. And behind that is the Captain, the Major, the Colonel, the generals and that guy sitting in the White House."

There was an uncomfortable pause. Then Plumb chuckled a bit and countered, "Yeah, but the man of the house has the house and the furniture in it and the food on the table and the car to go buy it with. Man, he's got a lot of back-up."

Howard stared at him. Then he looked back at The Newt for confirmation, for an argument, for anything. But no one said a word.

The Newt finally took a deep breath, but nothing came out but exhale. And The Rolling Plumb mumbled, "Hell, let's get back to the `Y'." The three turned like schoolboys and trudged back into town and to the little electric car commanded by a woman in spiked heels who barreled her wagon through the streets of Brest.

Howard wrote Ellie how "wife sick" he was, but for most of the letter he served as her Burton Holmes, the travelogue spokesman for everything from the castle that loomed over the City to the little street shops where barmaids passed drinks over mahogany counters like in "les Etats Unis." But he made it clear that he only "peeked in." He was keeping his promise not to drink.

And the shopping: 40 francs for Sam Browne belts—that was $7.20; "fore-and-aft" overseas caps for 20 francs in a little shop run by a fat old dame with a daughter and their little barking Pomeranian named "Yu-yu"; gold bars cost 1 franc and 70 centimes. Later, Howard took his back and had them embroider the insignia on his "fore-and-aft" be found it had more "swank". And there was the Breton insertion lace for Ellie's blouse and. skirt or coat, and the chemise yoke he hoped she'd like.

Dinner time: *"Cafe, mail pas, du sucre."* Butter? *"Il est defundu."* Milk? Cream? Cheese? All gone to serve the war. But plenty to eat, lots of what in America was called *Victory Bread.*

Out on the streets, a loud clatter scooted the trio onto the sidewalk in expectation of horses at a full trot. Instead, half a dozen kids galloped their way, wooden soles and heels clattering o. cobblestones all but drowning out, "Oh, les Americains! Les Americains! Geev me penny, give me penny!"

What a jumble! Khaki clad masters of destiny, part of an incredible organization capable of moving troops through sub-infested waters and securing them in a far away land of museums and leeches. Here they were, three warriors surrounded by begging urchins only a train ride from the war to end all wars!

"Hell or Hoboken by the first of the year!" Blackjack Pershing had said. Pride, fortitude and power were all heady stuff. But, God, how tragedy and farce do keep company!,

---

It was just five days after landing, on June 28th, when Ken reported: "Well, the rest of the Regiment will be here in.a week, and all we know is where we're going and that there'll be a school set up for radio and ground-to-air communications."

Howard glared at him. "You mean we were sent over here in advance to find out what's going on, and that's all we can tell Colonel Eckhart when he gets here?"

"And where are we going?" The Newt interrupted.

"Lathus, a little town near Montmorillon in the Department of Vienne."

Colonel Eckhart and the rest of the 351st, praised by the ship's captain as "one of the best behaved, best organized outfits" he'd brought over, had arrived in Brest and were boarding trains to Lathus. And they weren't *Forty-or-Eights*—these trains had wooden benches!

On Sunday evening, June 30, 1918, all trains stopped just for the night at the Pontanazin Barracks that Napoleon had built for his "levies." Pup tents sprouted, and thousands of khakied men—black troops and white officers—encircled the tiny brick buildings like bees on a honeycomb. That night, Howard wrote Ellie his happiest report to date, not a travelogue through ancient castles or picturesque portraits of trolleys, lace and french cider, but a dissertation on life in the military, the raison d'etre for sacrifices, deprivation, the rugged, turbulent times all dependent loved ones were schooled to visualize, recognize, respect. But, oh, how much fun it was!

Dearest Ellie Girl:

For the first time since Plattsburg, I'm under canvas again. A canvas tent in broad, green fields takes the place of our city hotel. My bed's an army cot. I've stretched out my lungs another inch in the fresh air blowing through camp in a half gale, and I've an appetite like a horse.

When "to the Colors" was blown, I felt a new thrill—or rather an old thrill newly returned. We were lined up in a street of brown canvas tents and beyond our street were other streets of other brown tents, row upon row. It was just so that I stood my very first Retreat, two years and a month ago, in Plattsburg.

Beyond the little road in front of our tent a hedge of sod with little dabs of purple from "the bonny burkle heather." I wish we could pick heather and cornflowers here, as we gathered violets and anemones and Judas-tree blossoms such a little while ago.

The sun is low behind the cliff. It's 9:00 P.M I have my heavy sweater on. I'm sleeping in my Kapok bag (a wonder—the equal of three blankets!) with two blankets under me and one over.

Taps and sunset! It's just like the old song. Now comes "the long, long night of waiting." But surely as tomorrow's sunrise, so surely there'll be the long trail's ending and best of all—Buddy and you,

Yours ever and ever, Howard

The next morning, on to Lathus!

Poor little Lathus! No one had bothered to tell them that a regiment of American soldiers would be arriving! No one in Lathus had ever seen an American before. Lathus had never seen even a French soldier before, except for the few who returned armless or legless after being "called to the colors."

When row upon row of railway cars pulled into town, the ancient Station Master was in shock.

"We're supposed to be billeted here," someone tried to explain in Pidgin English. The Station Master sent for M. le Maire.

Monsieur the Mayor, a fat little jacketed politician, arrived with his secretary, a very thin little man in a dusty gray frock coat who wore yellow leggings and hopped around like a sparrow, a monocle miraculously wedged between brow and a long hooked nose clipping a drooping mustache to his upper lip. His crown was a Sherlock Holmes hat with ear-flaps tied above, and over one shoulder and under the other arm was a hammock, too big for carrying books and too small to crawl into. In fractured French, he made it clear that he was very "precious of it."

Huge conference!

Freshly mowed fields would be the regiment's new home. Owners stood silently at the side. Friends of the owners, then friends of friends, and finally, it seemed, the entire town of Lathus gathered, ageless women and wrinkled men with assorted children, all silent, all watching.

An old teamster, his small son, a pony and a wagon with two bright-blue wheels hauled baggage from. the train to the stubbled, moist, receiving field while everyone argued over who would get the conveyance next.

"You know what day this is?" the Newt grunted as he unloaded the cart.

"Monday; isn't it?" huffed the Rolling Plum.

"The Fourth of July!"

"You gotta be kidding!"

Howard bad a sudden premonition that back in Massachusetts Buddy had just arrived.

Wet fields stripped of hay, newly planted with tent pegs, canvas and khakied strangers! Villagers stared and then straggled back to town. Mess gear clinked and rattled like cowbells while kitchens steamed with vats of hot coffee and canned food. Hours raced by. Hours crawled by.

A bugle called Retreat, not lined up in front of muddy streeted tents, but in an area reserved. Boots, boots, three. thousand pairs, marched by squad, platoon, company and battalion to the newly designated Parade Grounds,

The 351st band played the National Anthem. Music rolled over the fields and through the little town, Villagers returned, running full tilt, dressed in their best, carrying flowers.—great bouquets of roses stripped from gardens. Ceremonies done, Lathians encircled the colonel's staff, garlanding them with blossoms, effusive in their welcome, their deference, their veneration.

Poor Colonel. Eckhart! Hand over his heart, he nodded; smiled and tried to bow, standing before his three Battalions stiffly at attention. Then Howard's Battalion Commander, Major Harris, spotted him. Here in France, and still waiting for his silver leaf, Howard thought.

"Hey, Andrews! Get over here! Give the Colonel a hand. See if you can make out any of this patois."

"Bon jour, M'sieur. Comment sa va? Je ne parle pas le Francais bien, mais peut-etre je peut . . . uh, je peut . . . " Howard turned to Colonel Eckhart.

"What's the matter, Lieutenant? What's he saying?"

"Well . . . nothing, yet, sir."

"Then get something. going! Find out what he wants!"

"Que voulez vous, Monsieur?"

A massive. assortment of meaningless clipped consonants and nasalized vowels engulfed lowly Lieutenant Howard Andrews. He remained frozen, open mouthed.

"What's he saying," the Colonel insisted.

Howard stared at the rolly-polly Maire, now grinning in silent anticipation, his scrawny assistant, the hammock-festooned, yellow legged sparrow dancing up and around the Colonel, gesturing and babbling with mounting insistence.

"Damn it, Andrews, what the hell's going on?"

A loud, clear voice from beyond the Colonel shifted the focus. "Pardonnez moi, M'sieur, mais que je vous aider?"

Moving through the final rays of sun sliding over French hills, the figure separated itself from a group of eight and gently took the dancing sparrow's arm. As he passed Colonel Eckhart, Commanding

Officer of the 351st Regiment, he turned briefly to toss a soft salute but then, continued on with the sparrow to Monsieur le Maire.

Howard watched, transfixed. It was Boudreau!

No! With gleaming gold bar and crossed. cannons . . . it was *Lieutenant* Boudreau.

CHAPTER FOURTEEN

With lyrical Haitian charm, Lieutenant Boudreau romanced the delegation, thanked them for their reception', praised them for their roses, listened to their' entreaties and then returned to Colonel Eckhart, smooth as silk, to translate the mayor's welcome and, at the colonel's bidding, invite the citizens of Lathus to stay for a concert by the regimental band. The concert wound up with the *Marseillaise,* and everyone was delighted: In return, the Mayor invited the entire 351st to the Lathus celebration of Bastille Day, a little more than a week away.

Howard had watched Boudreau—he found it hard to think of, much less say *Lieutenant Boudreau*—traversing back and forth between Colonel Eckhart and the Mayor with his bandy-legged assistant dancing around the duo asking questions and.coachng tthe conversation.

Battery Commander Captain Lewis had moved over to the group of eight black officers and stood quietly, quizzing them, nodding his head occasionally. There were a few other captains and Field Grade officers there, including Major Harris, 3rd Battalion C. O., still waiting for his silver leaf

Howard wondered, how all this was going to play out, not the, least part of which would be his new relationship to Sergeant . . . that is, *Lieutenant* Boudreau. Superiority can be a fleeting thing, he contemplated, and, as Ken Hall had originally proffered, "Rank among lieutenants is like virtue among whores."

Howard need not have wondered how the new black officers would fit in with the 351st. They didn't. As assignments went out, back came complaints from company commanders who wanted no part of a black officer.

"Breaks down the morale," was one argument. "I'm not going to have them at my Officers Mess table," was, another. "How the hell am I going to be able to tell my officers from my enlisted men?" This one was told, somewhat sarcastically, to check the insignia.: 'But the men won't take orders from another black!" That was the main rationale.

The eight new second lieutenants remained on detached duty at Regimental Headquarters. Gradually the ruckus died down, and word surfaced that one was assigned here one day and another there the next, so it became apparent that times were, changing and things were not so clear-cut anymore.

Those first few days, while everyone was bobbing in and out of private homes, wined and dined, black or white, enlisted or commissioned, Howard wandered through town. In a jeweler's shop window he looked hard and long at a little chained locket. He thought of Ellie's tiny picture in his writing desk. Impulsively, he stepped inside and purchased the locket. Opening it revealed two matching frames! After a *few* seconds he thought, *maybe I'll get a picture of Buddy!* He tucked the chain under his collar and beneath his shirt so he wouldn't be out of uniform. *Now I'll have them with me wherever I go.*

"Lieutenant Andrews?" It was the familiar Georgia twang he'd known back in Meade.

"Hello, Chew! Good to see you."

"Lieutenant, this here man's wanting to meet you. He's a preacher, and he wants to invite us Catholics to his church this Sunday."

Howard shook hands with *Monsieur le Cure,* a huge, bubbling man who spoke just enough English to convince Howard that here was his first magazine feature!

> *. . . . A tall man, wreathed in benignity, good nature and good plump flesh, Le Cure was one continuous laugh. He started laughing when he saw you, he laughed uproariously when he greeted you and before you left him you were chuckling yourself like a tuning fork. I believe when he preached a funeral sermon the corpse sat up and laughed with him.*
>
> *He wore the regular black cassock with white ruff and the huge, broad, flat hat of the priesthood. If he had only been clothed in snuff-colored sackcloth with a rope about his waist and sandals on his feet, you might have taken him for good Friar Tuck.*
>
> *Le Cure took me to his home so I could let the men of his faith know how to find his church on Sunday. It was a big stucco house down. a little lane near the church, with a big brown-wood and white-stone fence about it. Rubbing his hands, laughing continuously, Le Cure called for the old dame who kept house.*
>
> *"Bring us wine," he bade.*
>
> *Now I was in a fix! Wine here is like a cup of tea; back home, and refusing it is an insult to hospitality. Nevertheless, I asked him to excuse me.*
>
> *"I don't drink wine,;" I apologized.*
>
> *"But what do Americans: drink?" he puzzled. Then he slapped his thigh and roared, "I know—beer!"*
>
> *I told him Americans drank everything that was ever corked in a bottle but that I'd like just a glass of water. That*

brought a laugh. But he called his old dame again and told her to bring some water, too.

"Water?" she gasped. "But why? Does he want to wash himself?"

"No," gurgled M. le Cure, "he wants, (he! he!) he wants to, (ho!. ho!) he wants to drink it!"

"Mais, pourquoi?." debated the crone. "When there's wine?"

Nevertheless, she brought a pitcher of water and stood by frowning in perplexity, watching to see if I really did drink the stuff or washed myself as she suspected I intended to.

Before I could pour, the old priest deliberately tipped half a teaspoon of wine into my glass. He then filled his own with the deep crimson liquid, cried, "A les Americains!" and drained his glass in one gulp.

I stared at the dark spoonful barely covering the bottom of my water glass. Then I put aside my scruples—and pledge of abstinence—and swallowed. He asked me if it was not good wine. It was excellent, and I told him so, and that brought forth a gale of approval. I had fulfilled the conventionality of hospitality, so he now filled my glass with water and poured one for himself Raising *his own glass, he said slyly, "A votre santé!"*

The water-was horrible!—greenish in color and saturated with sulphur. Here wall I, thirsty for a drink and ending up with a dose of Rochelle *salts!*

The French may not stand with one foot on a brass rail pouring down whiskey, but they do drink their wine. And the wine may have no more alcohol than grape juices but its better than what comes out of the tappet.

After you taste the water—as I did—and you still have to ask why they don't drink it, they'll tell you quite simply:

"Why? When there's Wine!"

Howard called his story "On the Wagon in France," sealed it in a manilla envelope, copied the address from a Liberty Magazine in the YMCA and deposited the envelope in the mail bag along with his usual quota of letters to Ellie.

During the days that followed, training took on a frenzy. Howard's writing desk stayed unopened beneath his army cot. Still absent was any word from home; the only letters from Ellie were the three he'd brought with him. At night, fleeting memories of her warmth sustained his lonely descent into the arms of Morpheus. Reveries covered the time she'd whispered, "Oh, Howard, do you want me still?," the gentle probing of their wedding night, arms that crept around his neck each day and, night, the feel of her body pressed against his, sometimes bulky with overcoats, but mostly body close. His flesh moistened in the fantasy.

Buddy didn't enter the picture.

The sun bounced gray skies onto the 351st tent city. Howard popped up in his cot, on the threshold of panic".

"My God, he's here!" he muttered.

Extricating himself from the sleeping bag and blankets, he reached under the canvas bed for his precious, inlaid writing desk. Inside was "The Buddy Letter."

Something had come to him in the night, in his dream. That something had been Ellie, and she was saying to him: "Howey! Buddy is here! Buddy is here!"

"July the eighth! July the eighth!" He kept repeating the words over and over to himself as he carefully edged open the third of Ellie' letters.

You're the dearest boy in all the world . . . it began. He raced through the pages as though they would actually tell him that he was now a father, that the baby was in his mother's arms and that Eleanor Arlington Andrews was safe and un— . . . un— . . . "un"—what? "Un"-harmed? "Un"-lost? "Un"-no-longer-his! The fear of loss welled unexpectedly. The pages themselves were lost in a wave of foreboding. The world sat on his chest.

Through the openings round the tent flap Howard could see the gray sky, almost as dark as the interior of the tent itself Three other comatose bodies filled the corners, rasping, sighs of night breathing underscoring his dread of the unknown. He lay back on his bunk,. the letter crumpled in his clasped hands, seconds passing between each brief gasp for breath Not moving, he stared at the canvas blackness until the world came alive with grunts, groans, arms an legs flaying about, boots, shirts, pants, jackets, caps, tent flaps untied and tied back, voices, bodies stepping gingerly over tent ropes, begrudgingly tromping through the muddy pathways and then, up ahead, the smell of coffee. Day was dawning.

All day, and all the next day, still no cable from home.

On July 11th, the regiment's "radio-triplets" were uprooted once again: Along with all the regiment's radio; telephone and communications operators and "specialists," they entrained for *La Courtine.*

La Courtine; Department de la Crease, home of the largest artillery school in France. A huge conglomeration of office buildings and billets offered the nearest thing to what Howard imagined would comprise a college campus. He saw to his trunk and bedroll and acquired directions for the quickest way to the town center of *La Courtine.* In short order, he found the cable office and wired Ellie. His panic had subsided somewhat, but he was still certain in his heart that he had become a father on July 8th. He was as certain as if *Le Cure* had sent one of his saints to show him their son.

On the 12th, he wrote his first letter in ten days. Sitting on his bunk, pen poised, he framed his writing desk bottle. Then he wrote:

I believe you'd let me know . . . I felt you were calling me . . . and I wanted to answer and come to you.

The pen dried. He scratched the paper a bit and then dipped the point into the tiny writing desk bottle. Then he wrote:

> *I have not received any letter or cablegram. You mustn't worry, for that's as I expected, although I didn't say so before I left. You see, I've been so much on the move that it would be hard for my mail to get to me. I have hopes, however, of getting some of your letters within a few days now—a week at the longest—for now I have a definite address which will not change for some time. Also, I cabled you this afternoon, telling you to wire me the Big News direct to La Courtine.*

He would keep anxiety a secret. He would continue to wait for the cable.

The following day he raced from morning class to the *La Courtine* cable office. There the old man handed him a greenish slip of paper, folded over itself to a mere two-and-a-half by five inch size, the outside flap labeled *"Republique Francaise Postes et Telegraphes"* and, in large letters, *"TELEGRAMME."* Beneath, almost illegibly, was the old man's handwriting: *"Lieut Howard Andrews La Courtine Creme."* And someone had added in pencil, "351st F A." Inside was the same outrageous handwriting, but the words. "Springfield" and "massachusset" and "Son eleventh,both fine Geo" were eminently decipherable.

Howard leaned on the counter. His son—Buddy—had arrived the very day he'd moved to *Courtine*. While he'd fussed with paper and pencils, with class schedules and books, his whole reason for being had endured the most profound experience of his life. Of her life, he reminded himself. He traced his actions and behavior that eleventh of July, calculating the moment it might have happened. Eventually, strength returned to pay the fee, and he stumbled back to the barracks and lay numb on his cot.

"Hey, Howey! It's time for class."

The Newt stood silhouetted in the doorway like a line drawing. Howard pocketed his cable silently and joined his companion lumbering down the hallway.

"Where were you for chow? I didn't see you there."

"I had to go into town." He pulled out the little green slip of paper and handed it to The Newt.

What were his feelings? Had he really been looking forward to Buddy? Weren't his letters filled with Buddy? He thought back. There was the locket with the tiny frame just waiting for his first picture. And yet . . . .

He went through his mental scrapbook of Ellie.

There was the kiss as he bent to say goodbye in the coach at the Baltimore station, the diffused picture of her face in the window as he ran along side the train. The anxiety.

No!

He returned to remembrances of the bedroom on the brief honeymoon, at Mrs. Stewarts, the nightgown with the little frills at the collar, their lying with faces so close that noses rubbed, eye lashes that flicked up and down as she smiled. The warmth, they privacy!

He wondered what Buddy would look like.

Classes continued every day, morning and afternoon, with lectures in the evening—the theory of electricity, the structure of batteries, the property of magnets, how to rig antennas (that brought back memories), how to communicate with aeroplane spotters using colored panels. He was becoming an engineer, a fragmenter of time and fact, a disciplinarian: All the freedom to do what he wanted to do, write what he wanted to write, dream what he wanted to dream, was being sublimated by this disciplined routine of classes that began with a huge cannon booming three times at 5:30 a.m. and ended at 9:45 p.m. when candles were extinguished and letters to wives concluded. These final hours in the evening were the dividing time, hours of creativity, of letter writing, when he submerged himself in thoughts of Ellie and Buddy.

For there were now two Howard Andrews. One was the evolving expert on "auto-transformers" and the "counter electric force," the growing side, the side that saw himself shine in classes where he never dreamed he could excel. "Tuning in A-1 Set," grade: 99; "Four Types of Ariels," 16 out of 20, "Audion Bulb," 30 out of 30, "D.C. Voltmeter," 5 out of 10, "Liaison for Adjustment by Aeroplane," 20 out of 20! And on it went accolades in an area hitherto unknown to him. Life of constant affirmation and glowing reports. Heaven! War was fun!

But then there was still the other Howey who resurfaced in those sublime hours of candles and creativity, hours when the happy but hapless newlywed daydreamed of Ellie and a healthy, baby boy. Why a boy? Because it couldn't be anything other than a boy. He had willed it. He had created it. The creative Howey, the father, the lover, the writer.

Howey had essentially split himself in two with soldier-engineer on one side and lover-creator on the other. Of course, the engineer would be. sublimated once the soldier saw action, a demarcation that would occur when the regiment moved from Service of Supply into Zone of Advance. He would then again be simply Howard the soldier. The lover-creator would remain on hold till the end of hostilities, but then love would triumph and fill his world, not just in letters but, waking or sleeping, Ellie would fill his world.

A stunning afterthought revealed that there would be a further split when the fruit of his loins separated him from his "Belovedest," the lover from the father. He was like an amoeba, splitting and splitting again. Was that what life-offered, constant bifurcation? He liked the phrase. It sounded funny—erudite. But it panicked him to think that just when he had a handle on life and marriage and self esteem, here he was breaking up into little pieces. Worst of all, he was obliged to establish, maintain and forthrightly rule over each element in this hodgepodge of responsibility. How? How?

Weeks passed, and test scores were tabulated. Records of achievement were added to his 201 file, train tickets back to *Lathus* were handed out, trunks loaded, and back they went.

"Well, did you learn anything?" Major Harris' welcome-back made him feel like he was more of a distraction than a returning hero. "Got some changes for you. You'll be Assistant S-2. Intelligence Section. Don't disappoint me."

What a break! Beginning to catch up with Ken. Maybe First Lieutenant Howard Andrews won't be far off.

Newton Deihl Baker, Wilson's Secretary of War, announced that there were now one million American soldiers in France and a second, third and fourth would not be long in coming. *Soisson* fell to the British, the French Cavalry rode down fleeing Boche and newly arrived Americans were licking the tripe out of the Crown Prince's own pet Prussian terrors. Another large manilla envelope was off to the New York Sun:

> *We have long passed the stage where Germany's superior man power remains to be counterbalanced by our troops. Every American soldier who lands in France helps tip the scale. The sooner a successful offensive comes the sooner comes victory.*

He wondered if any of his reports to the Sun would ever be printed. And what about those articles for the Post and Liberty? Oh, well, they'll probably take a long time to answer, and this is certainly going to be a long war.

July 18! *Whoops!* There were five letters lying on his cot. *Hully Gee!* He tore each of them open. *From my wife!* They were all dated June. Numbers at the top of the opening pages were 2, 3, 6, 7. And then there was number 8, the one saying she'd received his cable from *Brest.* Now, a month and a half since he'd left Hoboken! *But they're here!* Not all of them: not the first and the fourth and fifth ones, but there were FIVE!

He devoured them, over and over, and he sat right down and wrote her every scintilla of feeling that coursed through his body. He was ecstatic. The feeling was so great it was almost worth being half a world away just to feel this good.

For the first time he heard about his own father. George Andrews had sent Ellie a hundred dollars—a loan! It was hard not to appreciate that. He wondered if he shouldn't thank him. He'd repay it fast, as fast as his army pay would allow. He preferred the protective circle of the Arlington family over his own.

The following day he used his lunch hour to send a cable saying the letters had arrived. He chose the "soldiers' rate" with the cable sent to London and then held until after the slack business hours following the week-end rush. That would be 6 cents a word over the regular 25 cents. He figured that even the full rate would probably be delayed by urgent official business. Communication with America was almost as complicated as artillery spotting!

"Lieutenant? Here's the letters you have to censor."

Howard looked at the sergeant a moment before taking the stack hesitantly. "You mean I have to censor these?"

"Yes, Sir. All the officers of Battalion Headquarters have to split up the Headquarters Company Enlisted Men's mail. You been gone so long, we're just catching up with you. Be sure you write your name and rank on the envelope before sealing them."

"Seal them?"

"Yes, Sir. They have to be sealed before they can go to the post office." The sergeant looked at him as if he shouldn't have to explain such things.

Howard took the four-inch-thick packet back to his quarters and propped himself up on the bunk. Each envelope was unsealed.

The first one was a single sheet of the same paper he'd been using, large, yellowish onion-skin. The hand writing was large, clean and very precise.

> *I take my pen in hand to tell you that I am well and hope that by the time these few lines reaches you they will find you enjoying the same good health as they leaves me at present and having no more to say at present I will close these few lines."*

Howard carefully folded the paper, reinserted it in the envelope, wet his forefinger and spread his spittle over the gummed part of the flap, sealed the letter and then wrote on the upper corner of the envelope, "2nd Lt. Howard G. Andrews, 351st F. A., A. E. F." Then he sighed and turned to the remainder of the stack.

Ellie's letters arrived all out of order, but finally they acknowledged that Ellie and Buddy were both all right. Pa had decided to take Ellie to the hospital at ten the evening before Buddy was born, but she made him wait in the old Hupmobile while she wrote a letter on the little table in her bedroom.

The more Howard agonized over their separation, the more he reveled in his happiness. He wrote Ellie that she had more spunk than the soldiers he was serving with and that she should get one of their medals. He was convinced that he had the best of marriages.

"I found a book by. Jerome K. Jerome about a family, a middle-aged Englishman and his children," he wrote her. "'They And I,' it's called." And he copied out passages in long hand:

> *. . . When Love's frenzy is faded, like the fragrance of the blossom, like the splendor of the dawn, then will remain for you just what was there before—no more, no less.*
>
> *If passion was all you had to give to one another, God help you. You have had your hour of happiness. It is finished.*

If greed of praise and worship was your price—well, you have had your payment. The bargain is complete.

If mere hope to be made happy was your lure, one pities you. We do not make each other happy. Happiness is the gift of the gods, not of man.

The secret lies within you, not without. What remains to you will depend not upon what you thought but upon what you are.

Fools marry thinking what they are going to get out of it—good store of joys and pleasures, opportunities for self-indulgence, eternal soft caresses—the wages of the wanton.

The rewards of marriage are toil, duty, responsibility—manhood, womanhood.

Jerome confused him. Marriage was not "toil." It was love's promise of payment in kind, an affirmation of orderliness. He asked Ellie to sweeten her letters with assurances that their marriage was the secure haven he dreamed it was. He asked for validation and prided himself that he would find it in her words, in her love—even this far away. And he closed the letter with instructions to send razor blades and photographs enfolded in her letters.

Emboldened and full of purpose, he reached for his treasured writing desk, opened the top and then the special storage of fresh, awaiting sheets and turned to his other duty, the obligation to write, to become the soldier-writer from the front lines, to secure for himself the accolade of reporter.

Chapter Fifteen

As Howard struggled to maintain his equilibrium, once again the world crashed into his private realm. It was mid-October when Battalion Commander Harris called him into his tent.

"Pack your kits. You're going to Compiègne. Don't tell anybody where you're going and where it is, and don't ask me what it's all about," growled Major Harris. "It's all a big secret. Colonel Eckhart wants you and four other officers from the Regiment to go up there and find out what poisonous gas smells like. Smell it, sniff it, rub your noses in it, and after six days come back here and tell us what it does to you. Far as I'm concerned it's just one more way to die."

Howard was to become the 3nd Battalion authority on anything and everything transmitted through the air—radio signals, balloon observations, ground to air communications, and now gas. What surprised and pleased him most was that Colonel Eckhart had stipulated that he was to be in charge of the four other officers heading for Gas School, one from each of the battalions plus two from Regimental S-2. Obviously those French classes at CLI were paying off. Right up there with that good news was word that they were going right through Paris.

The trip wasn't as romantic as the expectations. The five shave-tails left Lathus at 5:15 in the afternoon, beginning a series of transfers virtually from city to city, changing from one train to another, passengers jammed into compartments and standing in the aisles or falling asleep astride stray suitcases. Howard found the Frenchmen talk of chivalry but seldom give up their seats on the railway.

The quintet greeted Paris at 7:30 in the morning, and there they had until 11 o'clock that night before a train for Compiègne left—fifteen hours they crammed with sight seeing, courtesy of a cab driver and his machine that appeared to date back to Henry Ford's first flivver. *Le Prix?* $3 an hour. Not bad when divided among five.

Off they went, down the Rue de Rivoli, past Jean d'Arc's golden statue to the Place de la Concorde, past the Tuilleries all abloom, past the Louvre, past the Place de Vendome with its tower made from canons captured in Napoleon's campaigns, past the Pont Alexander, III with its lamps and statues, along with dozens of other places he could barely remember when it came time to report his dizzying sensations to his Ellikins.

What struck him the most, however, was the Court of Honor, "crammed with souvenirs wrested from the Huns at the Marne, the Somme and Verdun," he wrote her. Everything from "tiny, toadlike trench-mortars to huge, cumbersome hideous looking Big Berthas." But what galvanized the visitors were the German airplanes and wreckage of the "Zepps" brought down by AEF firepower. Over in the corner was a biplane, the target-like circles decorating the wings covered, wing-tip to wing-tip with floral wreaths but, as he later wrote Ellie, "kept fresh and unwilted" by admirers of France's greatest air ace, the late Captain Guynemar, victor in over half-a-hundred dog fights with the Hun.

Howard and his A.E.F cohorts stood silent before the plane and its floral tribute. He promised in his mind and heart that one day he and Ellie would stand where he was now standing and remember why he had been here. And, together, they would tour the greatest city in the world. His promise.

Two days later the quintet was busy inhaling gas at the "secret" city of Compiègne. They sniffed and memorized the smells and all their names. The six days of school had barely ended when a telegram arrived from Colonel Eckhart ordering the five officers not to return to Lathus but to head for Bois le Prêtres near Pont-a-Morisson, "secret locales," where the entire 351st Regiment would be moving. As Howard wrote to Ellie, "We're through playing soldier, and at last we are getting into it." Out of the "Service of Supply" and into the "Zone of the Advance." The irony was that they were still kilometers behind the strafing, and only the maps reinforced the fact that they were into the "Z of A." To Howard it felt like they were still at Lathus—or even Camp Meade.

The Third Battalion, along with the rest of the 351st Regiment, was a lot slower in its move from Lathus than was the gas sniffing quintet in their eleven-hour train ride from Compiegne to the Bois in the "Z of A." They checked in with the Brigade Commander and proceeded to do absolutely nothing for days. His scripted comment to Ellie was, "It's a lazy war." He couldn't help but think of the phrase he'd learned when first he landed in the Army: "Hurry up and wait."

He didn't have to wait too many days before Major Harris led his battalion of eleven hundred men and almost as many trucks and towed mounts into the once quiet French countryside of Bois le Prêtres. In just hours it was tent city.

Second Lieutenant Howard G. Andrews returned the Present Arms salute of the Honor Guard stationed in front of Major Harris' pyramidal tent that served as both the Major's abode and

Headquarters of the Third Battalion of the 351st Field Artillery Regiment.

"Andrews!" The Battalion Commander had a voice that shattered glass.

Howard stopped cold. *How did he know I was here? I was just passing the tent. He has to have eyes coming out of his ears.*

"Sir?"

"Get in here!"

Major Harris' voice was as bad as his bite. Only the lowest private could hear his roar without a quiver. Privates expected it, but the higher the rank and grade, the less it was anticipated. Howard Andrews was right in the middle of the grade/rank format, and he responded to the command with appropriate speed concealing equally appropriate concern. He darted into the Battalion C. O.'s tent, saluting as he did so.

"Yes, Sir?"

"What are you doing?

"Well, Sir, I, uh, uh,—I—"

"Good. I've got a job for you. Get a personnel carrier—one of those Whites with the heavy armor—and high tail it over to Pont-a-Morisson and the regiment we're supporting and stick with them the rest of the day. S-3 is busy planning this move with the artillery outfit we're replacing, and I can't spare any of them. But I want to know more about the troops we're supporting, and that's what you're to scout out. I can't say anything more—and don't you, either—but get the layout there, so when our observers move up into the trenches they'll at least know where to go to take a crap. What kind of dugouts they have, what they can see, are the Krauts up close—and where? Up and down the line or just in spots? Get back here before twenty-three hundred hours. Now, move!" In a minute he checked himself. "Wait a minute. You're supposed to know French. What the hell does Bois le Prêtre mean?"

"Well, Bois means wood or forest."

"Where the hell's the forest?"

"Well, I guess this used to be one before German artillery took it down."

"What about Pont-a-Morisson?"

"Pont means bridge, so I guess it's somewhere near the Moselle."

"That's the river that runs down from Metz through Nancy, right?"

"I think so, sir. I don't know that much about this territory."

"Okay. Get going. S-3 can give you some maps, and come straight back to this tent. If I'm not here, I'll be in S-2 or S-3, so look for me there."

Howard threw a quick salute and raced out the door. He was double timing it to the Motor Pool when Captain Len Musgrave, Battalion Surgeon, literally bumped into him.

"Where the hell are you going? There a fire someplace?"

"Len, not now. The Old Man has me going up to the line to check some things."

"I'm going with you."

"Len, I said not now. This is important, now get lost." He started off again, Len hot on his heels. There was no shaking him, and while Howard was clearing things with the motor sergeant, Len was making the choice of vehicles with no prompting from anyone.

As Howard drove out of the Motor Pool, "Doc" Musgrave at his side, Howard asked, "How did you know to pick this vehicle?"

"Listen, I may be a doctor, but I know armor when I see it, and this White is the biggest, toughest batch of steel this side of a tank. Why do you think only the top brass gets to ride in it? And, by the way, did you know the White is made in Cleveland? That's my home town." He grinned.

Howard and Captain Musgrave arrived at Pont-a-Morisson, the little town behind the section where the Batteries would be set up. They parked the iron monster and trudged up the slope to the trenches to find troops from the 96th Division wandering from one point to another with apparently little sense of what was going on or that they were even involved in a war. The only clue was when men hit open terrain and hunched down on the run to the next dugout. *That's what happens when you've been in the line too long*, he mused.

The shock of finding how seasoned troops behave under fire was equaled by the realization of just who they were. The 96th Division! The black troops with their black and tan shoulder patches and the silhouette of a buffalo confirmed that the 351st had joined up with its parent organization, the division that General Pershing had formed to thumb his nose at the Kaiser. This was an historic moment, and Howard automatically began creating in his head the lead for his next contribution to the New York Sun.

"We joined up with the 96th, Buffalo Division, the famous black division which our 351st Field Artillery Regiment was created to support. A seasoned outfit, with reputable combat experience along the A.E.F. line . . . . " He'd finish the rest later. Then he mused, of course they'd be backing up the 96th. He was tempted to say to Len, "What other division would rely on the 351st?" but decided to hold his tongue.

It wasn't long before the two 351st officers were able to introduce themselves to Infantry officers in the battalion they would be supporting. They were anticipating—hoping, at least—that they, too, would soon be coming down off the line, and they couldn't have been more helpful in guiding their two guests around. It turned out that the trenches—all but the barbed wire that festooned them—had been property of the Germans, soldiers who had imagined these trenches were theirs forever. The present occupiers had driven the Hun out and across the fields to the wooded area where they now sat waiting for a chance to break through the withering crossfire with which A.E.F. machine guns greeted every bit of movement from the woods. Overhead they sent occasional strafing planes, again only to be driven back by American anti-aircraft fire exploding like popcorn around each sortie.

After creeping from one concrete dugout to the next and peering through the slotted observation points, Howard tested his bravery by standing up, full length, to look over the parapet out onto the field and wooded area hoping to see one of the dreaded Boche. But not for long. He loved giving himself the test, but he didn't want to be the fool who stuck his head up at just the wrong moment in time.

The Major who, like Major Harris, should have been a Lieutenant Colonel but had inherited a battalion without the rank, smiled as Howard stepped back into the trench. "You know, only two nights ago we were shelled unmercifully. One of those 'big boys' landed right on the edge of this same dugout, knocked a dent in that concrete there—four feet thick, it is—and tossed one of my men a couple of yards. No harm done, but gave the lad a bit of a scare."

It was late in the afternoon when Howard discovered his Battalion Surgeon companion, Captain Musgrave, was missing. He soon found that he'd gone off on his own and was reconnoitering Pont-a-Morisson where they'd left their vehicle. Howard clambered down off the hillside and went looking.

As he moved through the streets of Pont-a-Morisson, the sun dipped low behind the buildings. The town was a bizarre amalgam of soldiers from the 96th who were there to see that all was clear as well as townspeople returning to their homes Clear it was, but the Germans had left havoc in their wake, bureau drawers dumped out on the floor where Huns could ransack the French belongings before escaping the town. Gaping holes in walls and roofs gave evidence of the bombardment inflicted first by the Germans and then by the Americans driving them out. Amongst the chaos and debris, Frenchmen and their families picked their way homeward to deal with whatever had been left of their town, their homes, their lives.

"You know, it's getting dark. We'd better be getting back to the Major. He wants me there by eleven o'clock."

"Yes, it is dark," Captain Musgrave mumbled, gazing around at the havoc. He turned back to Howard, a strange, lost look in his eyes. "Let's go," he said simply.

"What's the matter?" Howard asked.

The Captain again gazed silently about for seconds and then returned to Howard, grimly. "It's hell, isn't it?"

They were silent as they trudged back to the armored carrier that would take them away from the real "Z of A."

Later, Howard carefully inched the personnel carrier down the dark roadway out of Pont-a-Morisson by the light of the moon and stars. Headlights were *verboten* this close to the lines, and towns were few and far between. At the first sound of another vehicle they pulled over to the side and inched the iron monster carefully forward till the stranger passed. More arrived and went by until the fading sound of one vehicle masked the arrival of another, and they almost pulled out into the pathway of an oncoming truck. A caravan loaded with troops passed while they sat silently waiting for the road to clear. And then they moved out. And then it happened.

Crash!

A three-quarter-ton truck tore into the personnel carrier, and wheels and axles went flying. The Captain had slid down onto the floor, and Howard found himself crunched against the steering wheel, staring into the front of a three-quarter-ton with two frightened black faces staring back, only inches away.

Howard and Capt. Musgrave climbed down gingerly and went to the driver of the truck and his companion.

"Are you all right?"

"Yes, Suh. I think Joey, heah's, a bit hurt."

"Can you move?" The surgeon began to examine the two men. "You feel all right?"

Again, "Yes, Suh," this time from both of them.

The noise had been earth-shaking, and it wasn't long before another vehicle pulled up and two other men stepped out of the shadows.

"Sam? Joe? You all right?"

"Yes, Suh, Lieutenant. I just didn't see them, and we was trying to catch up, and so when they—"

"I told you to keep the line closed up. It's a wonder you didn't get killed. You can't fall back that far and not—" At that point the speaker got a full view of the truck. "Oh, my God, this is a total wreck." All the personnel carrier had was a bent fender. He turned to Howard and Len Musgrave. "What in hell were you guys doing with that personnel carrier?"

There was a pause. Howard spoke first. "Good evening, Lt. Boudreau."

Boudreau took a quick breath and responded cooly, "Evening, Sir." Then he added, correcting himself, " . . . Lieutenant."

Howard noted wryly, "The Lieutenant used to be my Platoon Sergeant." The Captain reached out. A white hand grasped a black hand, and two khakied arms linked the officers. The symbolism didn't escape Howard, but it was a wry smile that masked his uncertainty as he added to no one in particular, "And we knew each other back in New York."

Then he turned with a grin to Boudreau. "What are you doing out on a night like this?" He hoped the smile penetrated the darkness.

"The whole battalion moved out of 'le Bois' hours ago. Apparently orders came down from Regiment to get into position when it got dark. I heard there's going to be a monster attack on Metz in the next day or so, some time before mid-November."

Howard began to suspect he was heading into trouble. "Where's the major?"

"Harris? He's up ahead in one of the personnel carriers. I raced back here when someone radioed me there'd been a crash."

"Gawd! You going back there? I'd better get to him fast." Then he turned to Captain Musgrave. "I told you we were going to be late."

"Relax, Lieutenant. You're not late. He's just early. Come on. We'll follow the Lieutenant up to the front of the column, and you can be so smart you found him even after he wasn't where he said he'd be. And in the dark, too. You may even get a medal."

Howard wasn't sure Len wasn't trying to be funny, but he almost took the last comment seriously. He turned back to Boudreau. "Head on, Lieutenant. We'll follow you."

"I think you can call me Hermes, . . . " And here he paused a bit and then added, "Howey." Again, a slight pause. "Hermes is my first name. It means . . . . "

Even in the dark Howard could see the grin on Boudreau's face. "I know what it means. It means 'Messenger of the Gods.'"

Len let out a guffaw. "God, that's apt."

Howey grinned and added, "And the god of roads, commerce, invention . . . cunning and theft."

It was Boudreau's turn to laugh, now. "I wonder if my Mamma knew all that was to come."

Then it was Len's turn. "I'm standing here with a bunch of dictionary addicts. Let's get moving."

"You first," Boudreau called as he headed back for his own vehicle. "If we run into anything, I'd rather have you two make the first contact."

Howard and Captain Len Musgrave caught up with the Battalion Commander where the line of vehicles had stopped in mid town. He apologized for not getting back as ordered, but the Major cut him short.

"Hell, Lieutenant, it's still not 11 o'clock, and the Colonel ordered me out long before you could have gotten back, anyway. No time to worry about that at this point. I've got at least one battery to move into place before the sun's up."

Before he could finish, the Battalion S-3 was on them reporting progress.

"Sir, I've got all three Battery Commanders heading into position. We're putting the on-line outfit into the bunkers as planned, and the other two are setting up a reserve camp just west of the city. We have a place picked out for one of them to dig in just down the line before sunup, and the other battery will stay back in reserve."

"Thanks, Captain. Have you talked to the Infantry on the hill?"

"Yes, sir, the Major says 'Welcome' and the sooner we can pull him off the hill the better."

"Well, tell him we're the artillery, not the trench jockeys of this war, but we'll give him the best blanket of firepower he's ever seen when the big day comes."

"Yes, sir," and the Captain was off in a run.

"Sir, what's that?"

"What's what, Lieutenant?"

"The 'big day' you mentioned."

"Son, we're going to clean the area from here to Metz, and when that's done the A.E.F. is going to march into that city and sweep out the Hun like dirt trash."

"So, we are going to attack, just like I heard."

"Attack, son, is putting it mild. We're on our way to Berlin."

Chapter Sixteen

Howard raced down the street of the little town, muttering under his breath, *"Damned letters! Damned letters."* Accusations bounced back at him like billiard balls. *Well, if you didn't want to be late, why did you have to start writing?* Another guilt trip. *It's not Ellie's fault you have to answer her letters just when you see a pad and a pen. Don't blame her for your being a frustrated journalist.*

Ellie's letters were the be-all-and-end-all for Howard. Not because he thrilled to accounts of the Arlington family back in West Springfield, Mass., but because they triggered the mountains of editorial comment only a frustrated writer could come up with. When he was not telling her what he knew she *must* be thinking, he poured on lavish sentiments over what she *should* or *should not* be thinking. He was her informant and her editor, all in one. And his letters covered every conceivable angle of what his wife, and now his child, *should* or *should not* like or dislike, do or even think while he was off riding the War to End All Wars

It was 7:00 a.m., and at this moment he was supposed to be at Battalion S-3, but he hadn't been able to restrain himself from babbling on paper and showing off for his Ellikins. *How many letters did he get this morning? How cleverly he knew just what she was going to write? How brilliantly he could respond?* No one could beat up on Howie like Howie, himself.

Howard ducked into the dry goods store and through the door to the back room where the night shift of First Battalion, 351st Regiment of the 96th Division was just wrapping up for the day shift.

"Where's the F.O.," he panted. A weary lieutenant looked up from the pad of papers and pencils with a baleful eye and drawled, "C Company. The bunker just left of the busted latrine."

"Thanks." He started out the back door.

"Hey, wait. Don't you want the briefing?"

"I'll get it on the hill," he panted. "Oh, who is it?"

"Lieutenant Boudreau."

"Oh, God!" Howard was out the door and heading up the hill to the front line.

He found Boudreau and settled down, brain and all. "What's the situation?"

"Quiet. There is no fire since chow time last night," he added in his lyrical Haitian dialect.

The two took turns peering out onto no-man's-land. The Germans were far away, beyond rifle shot. Only a shell could have reached them—or him, for that matter. In the back of his mind Howard mulled over Major Harris' words about the upcoming drive on Metz, the first step in the plan to take Berlin, the plan that would cut the heart out of the Kaiser and win the war. He was tempted to share the gossip with Boudreau, but that would sound like he was trying to act superior.

"What's for breakfast?"

"Oh, I donno, . . . Hermes." He paused a moment to reflect privately on Boudreau's first name. "I skipped mine this morning."

Boudreau took a quick look at Howard and said his goodbyes as he headed back down off the hill. "*Au 'voir.*"

It was a queer sensation, peering through the post's window-slit into the enemy land, realizing that off in the distance there probably were several Boche observers peering back in his direction and thirsting for a juicy target. Overhead, very high, a squadron of Boche airplanes attempted a flight into Allied territory. A battery of "archies" began polka-dotting the sky about them with white puffs of shrapnel and black smudges of high explosives until the Krauts became discouraged and headed back for Deutschland. Nearby, a flock of crows, aroused from the deserted fields by the noise of firing, flew about his head and returned to the feeding grounds.

As the strangeness wore off, Howard stood looking over the trench parapet at the distant towns and strong points Boudreau had pointed out to him. What did this strange, quiet scene have to do with the war? With men charging with fixed bayonets? With some room in Berlin where the Kaiser had to be measuring his chances?

"*C'est fini! La Guerre, c'est tout fini*! It's over! The war's over!" Boudreau's unmistakable accent trumpeted along the hillside as Howard raced to the emplacement's rear portal. Boudreau was half way up the hill, calling up and down the line to officers and men gaping open mouthed. Then his eyes met Howard's.

"The Germans have surrendered. It's over," he howled. "We've won! The war is over!"

"What the hell are you talking about? The Heinies just flew over a minute ago."

"Yes, but yesterday they came through the lines and asked for an armistice. They've lost Dixmude and Leus, Bulgaria's surrendered, Turkey might as well and the same for Austria. They've no one else to help them. They're quitting."

"What the hell are we supposed to do?"

Boudreau took what seemed to be his first breath since starting up the hill. "Well," he gasped, "the Major says they were given a set of conditions and sent back through the lines."

"Well, hell, then it's not over."

"Oui, but they'll have to quit. There's no more army. The Major says they have thirty-six hours to make up their minds, and then we'll agree."

"Well, then it's certainly not over. They aren't going to agree to anything we say. They're just stalling, and they'll probably come out of those woods guns blazing."

Howard turned on his heels and stomped back up the trail into the command post leaving Boudreau open mouthed, staring at all the faces gathered around.

Howard peeked over the parapet, convinced that the Boche would be pouring out of the woods any second. Then he darted from one emplacement to another shouting for them to "lock and load," get ready for the onslaught, because it was coming. "Don't believe any of that hog wash. The Heinie will never give up. It's a trick."

The rest of the day inched along with nothing new added to the gossip and rumors. Chow that night was strangely silent as though one ear was cocked for alarms of attack and the other for more news of an armistice. The sun settled behind the village of Pont-de-Morisson, scarcely a sound coming from villagers or the troops, waiting, listening for what they had no idea.

The sun disappeared, traversed around the globe and, hours later, popped up behind the German lines, lines also as strangely silent as those housing the A.E.F. So quiet. So deadly. P.F.C. Chew stood holding the tent flap in the dim light of morning, waiting for permission to speak. Captain Musgrave was the first to spot him.

"What's happened?" he barked.

Howard bolted upright.

"The Germans refused."

Howard swung his feet onto the dirt floor. "I knew it," he growled. "I knew they'd never accept."

Chew hurried to leave the tent, and hastily added, "Oh, and President Wilson has been shot."

Captain Musgrave gasped. "Been shot?"

"Three times," Chew answered. "By an assassin. It came over the wire."

"That's a crock," the Captain growled.

"May be," Howard agreed, "but I'll bet the German's refusal is true."

"May be," the Captain mumbled after a long, uncertain pause.

Up on the line, every gun kicked as fast as it could be loaded and reloaded, from the first meal to the last, a day filled with artillery barrages and infantry sorties. Line straightening, it was called.

By evening mess the rumor about President Wilson's assassination was debunked, but still no word on the Germans and the Allied conditions for an armistice. Once again the sun settled behind the tense little town of Morisson and made its way around to the German side. And once again P.F.C. Chew appeared at the tent flap, only this time he threw it back and belted without permission to speak.

"C'est fini. Ils ont accepté. La Guerre, c'est fini."

Howard and the Captain both let out a whoop and shot out of the blankets and bunks to dance a jig on the dirt floor of France.

A phone call had come this time, the Germans had, in fact accepted the terms and the armistice was to go into effect at eleven a.m. this morning, on the eleventh day of the eleventh month of the year 1918. Glory, Glory Hallelujah.

And there was a rider to the official order. The war was to end at 11 a.m., but at 10:56 every gun on the entire A.E.F. front line was to fire one round. One round only, but a line of rounds all aimed at an enemy that had reeked havoc on the rest of the world. It was an order that was meticulously carried out.

Howard described the event in his sixth letter of that month of November:

"At 10:56, just four minutes before the Armistice began, every gun on the whole American front line was ordered to fine one round. It was great stuff—the roar that went up from our artillery on the second of 10:56, and the shower of shells that went with it must have scared the liver out of Heinie. We gave them a sporting chance, you see—four minutes in which to answer our fire—but not a shot came back. In fact, the Boche in our sector did no firing all that morning. Too busy celebrating. But we wanted to show them that we were anxious to keep the game up and would gladly do so if they changed their minds about wanting peace so quickly."

Not so at Riverdale, however, as Ellie's 89th letter written that very day, Monday, November 11, 1918, reported.

Monday, Nov. 11, 1918
Blessed:

Last night I wrote, "It's coming," and this morning it came. It's almost unbelievable that this thing which has been menacing the whole world has been stopped by a mere signing of a paper, and that we here in America should be rejoicing only a few hours later. If I could only know you are safe, dear. That one thought is deeper than all rejoicing. If I could only know. But I just must have faith or I never could live, and I know more letters will come soon. Dear Boy, what an experience this has been for you. And to think of being right there when the wonderful thing was accomplished. I can't quite grasp it yet. The war is over! As I look back to what we had to face that last day together, is it any wonder that this seems a miracle? This will be a glowing Thanksgiving even if our loved ones can't be home with us, for we know they are coming as soon as they can be spared now. To think that my prayers should be so abundantly answered.

Dear, Buddy and I knew about it first. The bells and whistles in the city woke me at four o'clock, and when I called to Maude in the next room Buddy heard me first. Oh, there never was a second's doubt as to the meaning of those whistles, dear. In a jiffy the whole house was awake and listening with more joy in our hearts than we had known for months and months. I took Buddy over in bed with me, for I felt that I just had to have my arms around him. Dear little Buddy, asleep in my arms. How little he knew how much it meant to him and to me.

The city went mad today. Dad and Maude went to work this morning, but there was nothing to do. All the working people thronged the streets in all kinds of ridiculous costumes, with every conceivable noise-producing instrument and each and all throwing powder and confetti.

Dad came back for me a little later just to see the doings. The streets were ablaze with flags and crowded with autos, almost every one carrying a rear attachment of old tin cans and scrap iron. Some organizations had small impromptu parades, and lots of private cars were rigged up with effigies of the Kaiser or the Kaiser's Goat and fitting, printed notices hanging from the sides.

I stayed in the office and could see beautifully from the window. It reminded me of the way we watched the parade in Baltimore, dear. Only there was nothing organized and formal about this, just a yelling, screaming enthusiasm and a hideous din. All day it's lasted, and now at eight this evening it's wilder than ever.

There's a big jubilee down here in West Springfield tonight, and the folks have all gone down. Mother offered to stay with Buddy, but I had had the afternoon and just wouldn't listen to her. Dad had decorated the car with big straps of bunting and flags, and someone had a huge piece of sheet iron and a hammer. 'Nuff said! I can hear the racket way up here with all the doors closed.

Buddy is peacefully sleeping upstairs in the dark. If I could only make him understand. Sometimes it almost seems as though he did, the Precious, for he laughs and laughs whenever I say, "Daddy come home."

I'll never forget this day, Nov. 11th, the end of the war. Buddy's four month's birthday and his first short dress! What a combination of associations!

Tomorrow is going to be a legal holiday all over Massachusetts (Victory Day) and they are going to have real parades and sure enough celebrations.

Of course it's only natural to celebrate and as wild with joy, but somehow I can't rejoice that way. I don't know whether it's because this has all gone so deep or because my happiness is too sacred a thing to be flaunting before people. Last year I would have been as crazy as the very craziest, but tonight I just want to get on my knees and thank the dear Lord who brought this about. It's not only my whole life, but Buddy's.

Dear, think of going to bed tonight knowing that this great World War is over and my boy is coming home to me. Not right away, Blessed. I'm not foolish enough to think that—but I can at least think of our anniversary, as you once promised, can't I? I don't need to tell you I am happy, dear. I wonder if I have ever been as happy in my life before. But I know a happier time is coming when you will put your arms around me and never, never leave me again.

Love from all our people, dearest, and all the love of my heart from

Your Wife.

Chapter Seventeen

For all of his protestations to Ellie and Buddy about getting home, Howard, nonetheless, put in for leave as soon as the war was over on some far fetched supposition that he might get to visit more of France before returning to the States. He thought of the wonderful sights he could reconnoiter and then, one day, bring back Ellie to visit—his eight weeks with the victorious Allied Forces in the War to End All Wars.

The invitation for all AEF officers to request leave was widely promoted throughout the regiment. It was the Allied Army's way of offering a tantalizing reward but, at the same time, give the officers something to occupy themselves while suffering delay after delay in getting a ship to take them home. But in true Army fashion, those who were granted such leave were few and far between.

The few and far between didn't include Howard, and so he found himself relegated to keeping one platoon of Battalion Headquarters Company occupied with constant drills and repair work on the little French town now welcoming its original citizens back. The drills seemed senseless now that the war was over, and all the help in the world couldn't set things aright for the French whose homes had been invaded by the Germans almost three years earlier and now by *les Americains.* Roofs were torn off, walls had gaping holes, and jewelry and keepsakes were ravaged.

M. et Mme. Paillot were host for Howard's Battalion Commander, Major Harris, plus a handful of his staff, including Howard. Mme. Paillot would greet each remaining relic of her pre-war existence with a kiss, a caress and a *"Bon jour, bon jour"*——chairs, tables and the fireplace included.

M. Paillot was a bit more philosophical, being an eighty-year-old veteran of both the Maximilian War in Mexico and the Crimean War as well as an ex-captain in the French Army in Africa, but his moment of anguish arrived on finding that his wine cellar had been looted by the German invaders, and his 1800-francs-worth of fine Bordeaux and *vin ordinaire* were gone. He never complained about his missing war decorations, the gaping aperture in his roof, and the jagged hole in his bedroom wall where, on the night of 15 April, 1915, a German shell had careened through the room, just inches from his head—he had commemorated the incident by writing the date just above the hole in the wall, and the writing was still there—but the loss of good wine was almost too much to bear.

Two weeks dragged by while Pont-a-Mousson gradually regained its pre-war status and charm, all the while tolerating the 351st Artillery Regiment virtually occupying the town. The American tradition of Thanksgiving prompted the commanding officer of the regiment to declare a holiday with a break from wood cutting, house repair, and, of course, the ever repetitive close order drill.

Howard and Captain Shons, Regimental Adjutant, along with Captain Musgrave, Battalion Surgeon, decided November 28th would be a good day for boar hunting. There hadn't been much activity in this regard for the past three years, and rumors indicated that *les sangliers* had multiplied several times over. Hoof prints covered the sod.

Howard wrote Ellie that he gave Chew, his Louisiana born, French-speaking orderly, the day before Thanksgiving off with instructions to "wander through the country and make friends with some native who could put him wise as to what to do and where to go." Chew returned that evening telling how he had gone to "a certain forest near here and had met a Frenchman who told him there were *beaucoup de sangliers* thereabouts." Chew and the Frenchman had "gone forth to see the hunting grounds, and before they'd gone far they almost bumped into a drove of pigs. The pigs ran away except for one old sow who must have had young, because she charged at them. The Frenchman killed her with a bayonet. Chew came home," Howard wrote, "several shades lighter in complexion."

The next day, Thanksgiving, Chew led the trio of officers to the forest but asked to be allowed to return to town. "To write letters," he explained, but he'd obviously had his fill of boar hunting. The trio had a good laugh, but the rest of the morning was much less rewarding. It appeared that *les sangliers* did their rousting about during the night, so that Thanksgiving morning they were all sequestered in their hideouts, sound asleep.

The disappointed hunters returned to Pont-a-Mousson late that morning without the pigs they had hoped would supply the Headquarters Company with a luxury evening meal. However, Major Harris had arranged with Le Maire to use the school room for a banquet. Fresh beef allocated for the previous three days had been saved up while the men unsuspectingly and unhappily dined on "canned willy." Come the noonday meal that Thanksgiving, therefore, they feasted on soup, garden vegetables, fruit, nuts, cakes, coffee and the three-days-supply of fresh beef. It was a sumptuous meal, war or no war.

During the cake, fruit and nuts, Captain Whalen rose dramatically and tapped a spoon to his canteen cup and called for attention.

"I have a bit of information I believe all of you will be interested in hearing." Calls for "hush, hush," "quiet," and "hey, shut up" were bandied about the school room. The captain cleared his throat a few times and turned to grin at his company officers before unloading the bomb shell.

"G. H. Q. has ordered me to get you fellows ready to return to the U. S. of A. within—a week!"

Probably half the town of Pont-a-Mousson must have stopped in its tracks on hearing the cheers, yells, cries, and general mayhem that followed the last two words. It's possible that some of the townspeople even saw the roof of the school dining hall float briefly in mid air before settling back down on its pinions. Such was the sound of glee from Headquarters Company, most all of them Louisiana Cajuns who'd been dreaming of the bayou since the day they'd been bustled off to Camp Mead what seemed to be ages ago. Grown men came pouring out of the mess hall pounding each other on the back and laughing till they cried.

The steady drizzle of rain couldn't dampen all expectations to hear further orders, perhaps to board trains within the hour. That evening the air in Howard's tent was filled with anticipation, small talk, more anticipation and more small talk.

The day after Thanksgiving cranked up a bit as every man had to check in equipment, uniform and, of course, souvenirs, plus all the weaponry from rifles to howitzers. Those items listed as "lost in action" had to be replaced so the men would look smart as they "marched down Broadway," a dream held half in jest and half in adamant expectation of what was felt to be just compensation for all they'd been through. But there was also the same old "policing," this time over every inch of land for miles around with full knowledge that not everything had ended up secured in its proper niche and safe from the prying fingers and eyes of youngsters who were yet unborn. They knew that, when hostilities and occupation ended, recollection of war and its dangerous relics would fail to reach new generations coming upon odd pieces of metal lying in the grass.

But Howard's thoughts were epitomized in his letter to Ellie on that Friday after Thanksgiving, his seventh letter for November, 1918, certainly a record for number if not content.

"Oh, Ellie dearest, I'm glad I'm coming home soon, because now the waiting's harder than ever. I want you so. I want our home so—you and Buddy and I. And I want to sit and read to you while you sew. Above all, I want to be able to hold you close, close and tight, for a long, long time, and never say a word but just sit and think how wonderful it is and how thankful I am that, after all, it has come out so. And now, you little darling Wife O' Mine, goodnight and happy dreams. I love you with all my whole heart—you and Buddy. Tell him I'll see him soon. And you, oh Blessed. How good the sight of your dear face will be to me."

Friday, December 13, 1918—Official Rumor: "Start from Pont-a-Mousson on Thursday for St. Nazaire in Brittany."

Wednesday, December 18, 1918—still haven't left—Howard and Ellie's Second Wedding Anniversary!—Official Rumor: "Change destination to Marron for a train to Le Mans near Paris for full regiment examination for cooties, scabies, etc."

Fact: Regiment begins march from Pont-a-Mousson to Liverdun, a small city situated on a crag overlooking the Mozelle where men buy post cards by the bag full.

Thursday, December 26, 1918, the day after Christmas—letter to Ellie: "Boarded a train for Couterne in the Department of Orne by way of Laval, Mayenne and Domfront. Every time we passed a train, the French crews stopped, left the engines, and went to a café for sardines and cider while we waited. It's only about 125 miles we went, but it was after midnight that our journey ended. The men went to billets, but it was too late for the officers to go to the houses assigned and wake the owners up to let us in. So we slept in the station, those who could find room on the floor. I borrowed two blankets and slept along side Len Lyons (that made four blankets between us, over and underneath). Got to bed (?) at 4 A.M. and got up at 7 A.M."

Sunday, December 29, 1918—still in Courtine. Mail arrives! Letters from Ellie plus a new Saturday Evening Post! And Howey's Christmas box! His first mail since December 17th. He wrote to Ellie:

"I carefully untied every knot as a patience lesson although I wanted to cut it and open the box quickly. Then I got out that best picture of you, the smiling one—it's on the table by my bed, the one I'm writing on now, but I propped it up in front of me—and examined the gifts. There was Nan's and Uncle's tobacco first, then Dad A's plug, then Charlie's pencil, the hankies and that tool-of-many-uses and the book of jokes from Maude (I read all the jokes because I couldn't wait, and I agree that the 'nigger ones' are the best), and although Maude assures me the hankies are 'for blow, not for show,' I'm going to keep them for civilian use because they're so much too good for this muddy Army use, while, as the for the little tool, I haven't had a chance to use it yet but I'm looking about for a bottle or a cigar to use it on quickly. These all came in little boxes, you know, and they were the most artistically packed little things I ever saw. That 'craft' idea is a dandy.

"Then there was Mother and Dad A's gift—the pillow—I had to blow that up, you know, to see how big and comfortable it is. It will come in dandy, not only with my bedding roll but on the train when we make our next overnight journey. It's fine.

"You see, I saved your gifts until last. After I'd admired all the rest I took out your little book of soap leaves in the little envelope (they're a dandy idea, Honeykins!) and the ink tablets (in the bottle that I can carry beautifully in my pocket on trips) and the can of Imperial and—last of all, though I'd been itching to look at it first of all, my pipe! Say, Honey, that's some pipe! Why, you Blessed, I never dreamed, when I wrote suggesting a pipe for Dad A's Christmas—a '3B,' straight stemmed and big—that I was giving you a description of the very pipe you'd get me. The fact that I suggested just that kind for Dad shows, doesn't it, that I consider it the best there is? It's a beautiful piece of briarwood and a nice shape. You're a darling! I found my name inked on the silver band, right away, and also inside the leather case. Oh, I can't lose this pipe, I know. I'm glad you gave Dad the picture of Buddy and yourself for Christmas, for I know he'd rather have that than a pipe, so he's best pleased. And me—I have both the picture and the pipe, so I'm doubly blessed.

"Of course I opened up my tin of Imperial, filled my pipe right away, and then sat and smoked luxuriously while I told your picture how good it was and how nice you were.

"Have I left out Buddy's gift? I didn't leave it in the box, however. It came out just before your own, dear, and right away I took off my old strap, put my watch on Buddy's, and I can tell you it's as fine and classy as can be. I like it, heaps. You're all such wonderful folks to give me all these things and—gee, I wish I could get my presents to you!"

Wednesday, January 1, 1919—"I expect to beat this letter home, for the Division starts tomorrow for Le Mans for re-equipment, after which it goes direct to Brest to wait for boats. We move a regiment at a time, each regiment staying twenty-four hours at Le Mans. Therefore, unless the usual delays in train service are far exceeded, our regiment ought to be on its way early next week. How long we'll wait at Brest I don't know, but it probably won't be long. And then—home, dear! Lordy, that's the sweetest word in any language to me now. It is to most all of us, in fact."

Saturday, January 4, 1919—"We were to have left tomorrow. Now we are informed that our old bugbear, insufficient transportation, is taking his accustomed crack at us. The trains that were to have taken us to Le Mans and thence to Brest have not shown up. It'll probably be Thursday before we leave, is the dope now. On Thursday, I expect that date will be advanced another couple of days and so it will go on."

Monday, January 6, 1919—" . . . prospects are that we'll leave here about Thursday or Friday for Le Mans, wait there anywhere from thirty-six hours to three days and then go to Breast. Oh, Honey, it's going to be so very many weeks, I'm afraid, before I can see you—and perhaps even longer before I can really come home for always. The waiting is so hard, but at least we can know that it must come to an end some time. We must surely be on our sea trip inside six weeks."

Sunday, January 12, 1919—"Tomorrow's your birthday, and after all the letters I've written promising to be with you on that day, here I am still five hundred kilometers or more from any ship and with prospects of departure as uncertain as ever. Lordy, dear, when will I ever get home?"

Monday, January 13, 1919—"You're probably just finishing the last of that big birthday cake. I'm so glad, Honey, that it can be all wheat this time, with heaps of icing all over it. Wonder who got the ring this time? Did you leave it for Maude? If so, my congratulations to Ray."

Tuesday, January 14, 1919—"It's 11 o'clock. The room's cold as a barn, because that orderly of mine apparently forgot to get me any wood today. Also, I want to catch a couple of hours sleep before I begin the guard duty at 3 o'clock."

Friday, January 17, 1919—"Tomorrow is our anniversary, the eighteenth, isn't it, sweetheart? Seven months I've been gone. And Buddy is half a year old. He must be big as all outdoors by now. And you—I wonder if all's well with you. Oh, confound it. I can't write any more along that line or I'll be tearing my hair. I was glad to give time and happiness to come here when there was a war on, but now I begrudge every minute I spend in this darned country. I wanna go home!"

Saturday, January 18, 1919—"A month since leaving Pont-a-Mousson, and if dawdling a month all the time isn't hard luck I'd like to know what is. Next, today we had three more 'shine' shavetails assigned to our company, making seven in all. The men are going around calling each other 'Lieutenant' now. Oh, Lord!

"We spent the day killing cooties. The men's blankets and such clothing as was not ironed out yesterday were put in piles and sprinkled with gasoline, after which the piles were left to fumigate for a couple of hours. I'm sorry for the poor fellows tonight, for it's no joke to slumber in a blanket soaked with gasoline. Too smelly.

"They also bathed. We had a big engine barn by the railway station, and there we rigged up a shower bath by hitching a lard bucket to a rope over a beam. Nail holes in the bottom of the bucket furnished the shower effect, and the bucket could be lowered to be filled when empty. All around we built a wire framework and stretched shelter tents to keep out the cold breezes and the inquisitive French people. Some of the men fully expected to catch pneumonia, they say. Well, a bath is worth the risk, I think, especially if one has cooties. Personally, I've never had them (I'm knocking on wood as I write), which is lucky because McAnne's bottle of 'Black Flag' powder never got any nearer the front than La Courtine and never was opened. If I'd ever got cooties they'd have found me entirely defenseless.

"We heard some dope today, but I doubt if it's worth much. It is to the effect that the divisional de-lousing officer was here today and, being vastly pleased at the regiment's work, declared he would see we got a train direct to the boat as quickly as possible . . . . when I see that train I'll believe we're going, but they'll have to put me on the boat and pull the gangplank in before I'll really believe I'm on my way home."

Sunday, January 19, 1919—Rumor: "The brigade is to start next Saturday. That means that our regiment should leave here about a week from tomorrow."

Fact (letter to Ellie): "Yesterday we finished the de-lousing work and it's our belief that the men are now clean. Only a few had cooties anyhow. And now, dearest, I have a treat in store for myself. Selfish? Perhaps, but it's only a bath. Such things aren't treats at home. We used to call 'em 'necessities' long ago, but in France and particularly in Couterne for us they are luxuries.

"You'll be terribly shocked to hear me say I haven't had one for almost a month. I got M. Thomment to heat me a basin of water, which is now before me growing cold. And I've set a huge blaze in the fireplace to warm up this big, chilly room. Now I'm going to put a shelter-tent half on the floor to catch the overflow, and I'm going to give myself some scrubbing.

Tuesday, January 22, 1919—"Next Saturday it will be just a month since we piled off the train here Christmas midnight and slept on the floor of the station. Several times before this I have written that I would be with you before you received the letter, but this time I'm going to promise again and, if I lose, I'll buy you a five pound box of nut chocolates. General Pershing was here at Le Mans this week and, apparently as a result of his visit, things are sprinting up to beat the band. We are to sail by February 2nd . . . at the latest I shall be in the States by the fifteenth. Isn't it great? I'm heaps tired, sweetheart, but oh so happy."

Le Mans, France, Wednesday, January 30, 1919—"This afternoon our division was reviewed by General Pershing. I suppose it sounds thrilling to you, but now that it's all over I'm so tired and footsore that I can't enthuse properly. I wouldn't miss having been reviewed for fifty dollars, but I wouldn't go through it again for five hundred just now.

"We knew yesterday that the General was coming today from Brest and would look us over. Yesterday we spruced up some more on our drill and marching (we needed it) and shivered at the prospect of 'pulling a bone' and being held for further training in punishment. This morning we had breakfast at the regular hour of

7 o'clock and then a light lunch (bread and jam and coffee) at 10 o'clock. Following which we hiked to the big field where reviews are held, a field over half a mile square, and arrived there at 11:00 on schedule.

"The general wasn't to arrive until 2 o'clock, but a little legitimate rehearsing was necessary, of course, if our whole division was to be put through successfully. So the division commander reviewed us first. That took until about 12:30 and then we formed in one line to wait. We waited.

"It was cold as seven refrigerators, and a nippy wind was blowing. The ground was an inch deep in oozy, clayey mud. In the course of the review my platoon and the commanding platoon of the other companies in our regiment all had to wade through a four-inch pond in the field, about ten yards in diameter. Also, the uniform being shoes and wrapped leggings, I had had to put on a pair of field shoes two widths too narrow for me. (My feet have spread to the dimensions of mud-scows since I came over here, you know. I suspect I'll never be able to wear narrow-toed shoes again and nothing less than an 'E' width will do.) All in all, we were a bit uncomfortable, and the men, stamping and swinging their arms to keep warm, were divided mentally like old Caesar and Gaul was—one-thirdly wishing the General would come soon, one-thirdly doubting if he really would come and one-thirdly wishing he would come so they could call it a day and go home.

"It was just five minutes after two that he came. The bugler played the flourishes and we all stood at present arms, officers at the salute while his gray car rolled across the field. Then he inspected every regiment, every company and battery, every platoon of the thirty thousand men there, walking in front of each line with a long wake behind him that was formed of Major Generals, Brigadiers, Colonels and the commanding officer of the particular unit he was looking over. You ought to have seen those boys stand at attention when he came along. However, that was only natural. As one of the men in my platoon put it during a period when the men were at rest while a regiment to our right was being inspected (he was referring to the arrival of the car)—'Hit's mighty easy to see dass someone in dat cyar higher den a cowpral.' To which another responded: "Uh-huh! Disyeh's one time when you sees captains an' even cunnels reely come to attenshun.'

"Well, the terrors of the inspection over, came the review. I wish you could have seen it, honey. It was really fine. Imagine regiment after regiment of infantry and artillery, seven in all, marching as only colored boys can march to a ragtime military band and kicking out their heels as though to out-goosestep the Prussian Guards. And the long, colorful procession of company colors and battery guidons, the regimental standards and the American flags sweeping finely by. It was far better than any mere parade.

"When it was over and we were double-timing off the field the outfits were turned over to the sergeants, and all officers reported to the General. He stood with us all in a circle about him and gave us a little talk—a sort of goodbye pat on the back before we left France. Then we went home. And that's all, except that we were so blamed tired we never could have walked that three miles to camp if it hadn't been that we knew dinner would be ready when we got there and we wanted that dinner because we were so hungry our stomachs all thought our throats were cut.

"Did you ever hear that song by Carrie Jacobs Bond (I think that's the name) called 'Just a-wearying for you'? I reckon I can paraphrase the verse that goes:

'Just a-wearying for you, all the time a-feelin' blue;
Wishin' for you, wonderin' when I'll be comin' back again.'"

Chapter Eighteen

The trip from Brest to Hoboken was a non-event as far as Howard was concerned. Not that it didn't happen; it was just best left unremembered. In the first place, it wasn't a converted luxury liner like the Leviathan—or *Vaterland*—that had brought him over. It was a small transport that had been hastily converted from a supply ship to a troop ship with hammocks slung from every available post below deck to accommodate enlisted men and bunks stacked four and five high and crammed into remaining spaces for the officers.

Then there were the hours spent flipping pages on a borrowed book or flipping cards in unsuccessful attempts to outwit the crew in every imaginable version and distortion of poker.

Finally there was the boredom of leaning over the side rail, watching the foam running along ship-side and searching the water for any sort of sea life that would attract and divert attention. Howard tried the rail routine for a few hours the first day on the chance he'd spy one of those flying fish he heard about from the crew, but then he learned that they'd seen flying fish on the Pacific and not on the cold Atlantic.

Mainly, however, it was the matter of letters. He'd focused on Ellie's over the months before, and he'd satisfied his creative urges with works of his own, but here he was with an absolute guarantee of no incoming mail and an equally guaranteed inability to mail a letter anywhere. How ironic that he'd arrive on the doorstep of anyone in the world that he'd care to write before the letter itself. And, of course, that one person he'd "care to write" was Ellie. How frustrating!

When they sailed into the docks at Hoboken it was almost as though their arrival had never been expected. The dock workers were just going about their chores, and the ship's crew behaved the same. But the passengers, officers and men of the 351st Artillery Regiment were in a daze. They crowded the "gunnels" and stood atop hatches to watch the ship as it passed through the harbor and nuzzled up along side one of the docks. They looked about as though trying to determine if those creatures dockside were really Americans and not just another bunch of "Froggies."

As the men descended the gang plank, officers quickly chosen were stationed along the pier, herding the men along the wooden planks toward a huge shed quickly filled with officers and men of the 351st. Once inside, Howard spotted a wall phone in an almost hidden passageway and made a dash and a lunge for the receiver.

"Alderson at 345 Riverdale Street in West Springfield, Massachusetts—and quick," he blurted into the mouthpiece. "No," he answered, "reverse the charges. Hurry!"

Seconds crawled by like hours, minutes like weeks. Suddenly there was a voice. "Ma?" he called wildly, "It's Howard!"

He could hear Mrs. Alderson calling to Ellie. "It's Howard! He's on the phone!"

"My God," he realized, "I'm home. I'm actually home!"

Buddy dropped away, his lips pursing in and out, making those funny noises, little burbling sounds, indicating either gas or regurgitation.

Ellie swung him over to her left shoulder and patted his back gently, waiting for the telltale response. And then it came, several long, baby belches. She smiled, patted him again and lowered him onto her lap. But Buddy had had enough.

There was a knock on the door.

"Who is it?"

"It's Maude."

"Don't come in. I'm feeding. What do you want?"

"Nothing. I just wanted to see how you were."

"Well, wait just a minute. I'm putting him down, now." She rose and moved over to the crib where she gently lowered Buddy and pulled the short skirt down over his knees. Buddy's eyes closed and opened and closed again. Ellie smiled and pulled the blanket up to his chin. Then she fixed her blouse and opened the door.

Maude stood still, peering over Ellie's shoulder as she said, "The mail came. You got one from Howey." Ellie snapped the letter from her hand and moved quickly over to the bed where she sat and tore the envelope open with her fingers.

Maude didn't move. Finally she asked, "What does he say?"

Ellie just laughed, "Ha! Wait till you hear this. 'Tell Maude I've seen horses in the Army that might have been twin brothers to the one she described—yes, and some that might have been his granddaddy. Hold together? They have to wear splints to keep their knees from caving in. Uh-huh! And as for her remark, tell her please that I'm tickled to death to have her keep 'a little spark of love still . . . '"

Ellie's voice stopped while her eyes skimmed ahead on the letter. Maude moved slowly toward the bed as Ellie began again, her voice slowly picking its way across the page. " . . . of love still burning for me—in a sisterly way, of course." Ellie looked up briefly and turned again to the page in her lap scanning it wordlessly.

From downstairs, Ma's voice broke the silence. "Come quick. It's Howard. He's on the phone."

Ellie pushed past Maude, still clutching the letter in one hand, the other grasping the bannister tightly, and raced down the stairs to find her mother holding the phone out, the speaker in one hand and the receiver in the other. Ma's voice was calm, too calm.

"He had to go. He had to leave. He couldn't stay on the line."

There was a shocked silence. And then Ellie asked, "What did he say?"

"He said he just got off the ship, and the train he's supposed to be on is leaving for New Jersey and Camp Dix. He said he'll call you again from there. But he wanted you to know that he is back in America. He's home."

Ellie repeated the words, "He's home."

Ma echoed the words again. "Yes, he's home. He's finally home."

Ellie turned and slowly moved back up the stairs, smoothing Howard's letter against her breast as she ascended step by step.

Maude was standing still at the doorway. Ellie moved past her, over to the crib and knelt down quietly and put her hand on Buddy's blanket. He didn't move but made little gurgling sounds. Ellie smoothed the blanket, saying softly, "He's home, he's home, Buddy, he's home."

Chapter Nineteen

Howard's patience was sorely tested by the reception—or lack thereof—which the 351st received on the Hoboken docks. He hadn't seriously believed that Ellie would be waiting there, discernable from the decks above, eager for him to race down the gangplank and envelop her in his arms, but he had at least hoped for more than just a few stolen minutes over a public telephone. And even those were denied him.

Men of the entire 351st were herded into a large shed in anticipation, they thought, of a march down Main Street, an anticipation that was engendered by their show for General Pershing back in France. What they received instead was a long and sweaty wait for a train to take them from Hoboken to Camp Dix. Shades of the final days in France!

It was at Dix that "processing" was to begin and end, they thought. Instead, there was a long, drawn out registration which covered everybody from the Colonel all the way down to the multitude of buck privates who made up the artillery regiment.

The brief phone conversation with Ellie's mother had only heightened the urgency of getting up to West Springfield. Finding an available phone in Camp Dix allowing him to continue that conversation and finally hearing the voice of his beloved Ellie was virtually impossible where thousands entertained similar fables. Howey and his surgeon friend, Captain Musgrave, enjoyed the same cluster of army bunks they had put up with in France except that they were now in wooden barracks instead of tents over damp, dirt floors.

"I've got to get up to Springfield," Howie fretted. "I told Ma we'd be through here in a matter of hours, and I'd be on the next train."

Captain Musgrave scowled at him. "What was that guff you said they told you about your records? They'd lost them?"

"No, they said they had a New York address and not one for Massachusetts. That's because I lived with my aunt up on West 105th Street before I was married. It was my last civilian address, so they figured I should be going back there. I guess they just want to keep tabs on me in case they need me again. Yeah, that's a big possibility. But I'm not taking Ellie to my Aunt Nana's because it's only a single room, and she has long since rented that out to someone else. And I'm certainly not going to have her kick him out."

"But they wanted you to go back to Manhattan?"

"Yes, and I want to go to Springfield. Idiots!"

Captain Musgrave thought about that for a while, and then he looked over at Howey with a half quizzical, half devilish look and suggested, "Why don't you just get on a train and head for Massachusetts. When they call your name out I'll explain everything, and when you get back to pick up your foot locker and stuff they'll have it all straightened out and your discharge papers waiting."

Howie's jaw fell, and he stared at the captain. "You'd do that?"

"Hell, yes, I might as well do one decent thing before I leave this damn army. What can they do? Send me back to France?"

"What about all my junk? And the souvenirs?"

"They'll be here when you get back. I'll stick around for a couple of days and keep an eye on them. Hell, nobody's waiting for me in Philadelphia, anyway."

This was news to Howey. He stared at the captain for a moment. "You know, my father lives in Philadelphia."

"Really?"

"And my baby sister."

"Well, you ought to be coming in sometime yourself."

"Don't hold your breath."

Howie kept his council regarding his feelings for sister Laura and their father. He figured he'd have to make the Philadelphia trip sometime in the future, and he might as well save those details for a time when they were absolutely necessary.

"Just be sure you're back in three days," added Captain Musgrave. "I don't want to spend the rest of my life chained to an army bunk."

Howie was at the Camp Dix train station and on his way to Massachusetts in minutes, stealing a few precious moments to make a phone call while changing trains in Hoboken. The result was the whole Alderson family waiting for him at the Springfield station five hours later with everything but the municipal band celebrating his return from "The War to End All Wars."

There was a lot of bed-swapping for those three days on Riverdale Street. Howie and Ellie were honored with the big double bed in the master bedroom. Buddy's crib was moved in, too. Ellie insisted on that. Howie wasn't too sure about the round-the-clock interruptions, but the nursing procedures piqued his sensibilities. As he watched her, he allowed himself to adjust to the expanded relationship of father, mother and offspring.

Ellie looked up. "We got a letter from your sister, and guess what."

"What?"

"They're calling their baby 'Bud.'"

"What! We got ours first."

"No, little Harry was born almost six weeks before our Howard. I guess we'll have to call him 'Howard Junior.'"

"The hell we will! He's 'Buddy,' and they can just change theirs."

"Howard, your language!" Ellie whispered. "Somebody will hear you."

There was a slight grumbling, but Howie recognized that he was going to have no authority over his bratty sister or her car-salesman husband. If they were going to call Harry Junior "Bud," then he'd just have to come up with something else.

"We'll call him "Howard Junior," Ellie offered.

"Not on your life," Howie argued. "We'll find something better. Besides, 'Howard' is my name. My kid will have his own."

"His birth certificate says 'Howard Junior.' You're not going to change that." She waited. But all Howie did was scowl and then turn away. Ellie proceeded uncertainly. "She also said they're expecting you at their house once you're through at Camp Dix. Your father will be waiting for you at the Philadelphia station if you call and tell him when you're coming in."

"Oh, Gawd! Everybody's trying to run my life already," Howie groaned. How was he to call Captain Musgrave about his going to Philadelphia? The chances of getting a call into Dix was worse than getting one out, he figured. Oh, well. He would simply tell the captain when he got back to Dix and then join him on his trip to Philadelphia.

Suddenly a thought struck him. "This might be the best thing that's happened."

"What?"

"I've been worrying over what to do with all the junk I brought back from France. I didn't want to bring it up here because of the time it would take to come back and get it when we find a place to live in New York. And I didn't want to dump it on Aunt Nana and Uncle Apsley up on West 105th Street, but that was the only option left to me. This way I can take it to my dad's place in Philadelphia and go get it any time we want after we're settled in. Philly is spitting distance from Manhattan."

"That sounds great," agreed Ellie. "And I'll get a chance to see him again. I'm afraid I didn't have much time to know him at the wedding. And, besides, Laura wasn't even there, so now I'll get to meet her and her husband Harry." She paused and added with a sly grin, "and, of course, little Bud Reitz."

Howie looked at her for a moment and then decided to share some of his apprehensions. "I've not had much of a relationship with my father since my mother died. I guess I never forgave him for dumping me on the Baptist Church and CLI in Suffield."

"Without CLI and Suffield, we never would have met," Ellie said gently.

Howie was silent a moment. "Yes, but that didn't make his dumping me forgivable."

"What would he have done with you and your sister and no one to take care of two young children?"

Again, Howie was silent. He nodded a bit and added, "That didn't make it any easier on me. And it was even worse on Laura. She ended up with one of my mother's sisters who treated her like a slave girl. I was told that one time she was locked in a closet with the dog for punishment."

"Locked in a closet?"

"Well," Howie drawled, "she probably deserved it. She was a pest as far as I was concerned. We all went back to Cumberland when I was about twelve, I think, and she ran around making enough trouble for six brats. I think some people over there still think I have more than one sister."

Ellie smiled. In a moment Buddy—or Howard Junior—was through, and she placed him gently in the crib before joining

Howard Senior. As they lay there, holding hands quietly, he couldn't help thinking that everything in his life, the war and even the family he'd come from was worth a moment like this.

Two days later he was back at Dix with Captain Musgrave. "That's great," enthused the captain. "The Philly train is pulling out of here at 1:04, and we'll have our junk all ready to load."

"And the discharge papers?"

"All signed and sealed."

"You're a real buddy," Howie answered, almost choking on the appellation. But he didn't want to get into that.

The 1:04 for Philadelphia rolled in and headed out on schedule, arriving at Captain Musgrave's home town at 4 p.m., also on schedule. Equally on schedule was Howie's father.

"Good to see you, lad," he said in his thick Scottish accent, gripping his son's arm and hand in as close to an embrace as each could muster. Howie knew that it meant "coming back alive" and dwelt on the logic rather than the emotion. The two of them went back to his father's home where Howie got permission to leave his things until he and Ellie were settled, and two hours later they climbed back into his father's car for the fateful trip to Wakeling Street and the bratty sister he hadn't seen since their mother's funeral.

Laura was on the doorstep with husband Frank and "Bud" just behind her. She came running down the steps and into Howie's arms. All the connotations of his "little sister" left him as they hugged each other, the neighbors peeking out of windows to see a soldier-boy come home from "The War to End All Wars."

Little Buddy—or Bud—ate his dinner in a high chair close to his mother who fed him between bites and chattered like a magpie. "How's your little boy? I understand you call him Buddy, too."

"Where'd you hear that?" Howie mumbled, taking a glance at his father.

"I think Dad told us," she chattered on with a glance at the old Scottsman.

Howie didn't wait for confirmation. "No, we don't call him Bud—or Buddy," he added quickly. "He's just Howard Junior."

Glances darted around the table, but all fell silent. Little Bud—or Buddy—gurgled and burped and giggled while his parents beamed.

Howie caught the 9:40 that evening for Manhattan and then the subway which took him to his Aunt Nanna and Uncle Apsley around eleven P.M.

"Heavens, boy, why didn't you tell us you were coming. Are you going to stay? I haven't said a word to Edward—that's the fellow in the spare room—but he'll be gone in a jiffy, and the room is yours. Why on earth didn't you telephone?"

Howie cut her off, the only way he knew to stop her. "I'm just going to spend the night, and I can do that on the sofa. I don't want you to kick Edward out. Tomorrow I'll have my old job back with the Sun, and I'll find a place for Ellie, myself and—the baby."

Nana looked at Apsley for a moment before answering. "Have you looked for an apartment before? I mean since you came back from France."

"Why?"

Nana didn't answer. She looked at Apsley for a split second and then said, "I'll go get the sofa fixed up for you to sleep on," and darted out of the room.

Howie stared at Apsley. "What's the matter?"

"Son, there's not an apartment available in the city since the war ended. Not even a hotel room. People are commuting in from Philadelphia and Peekskill."

Howie was stunned. After thinking a moment, he mumbled, "I guess I'll do the same. I can stay with Dad in Philadelphia till I find a place." Then he added, "But I don't want you to kick Edward out. The folks down at the Sun will have connections, and I'll find something in short order."

If the housing situation was bad news, his reception at the Sun was a disaster. All the jobs had been filled, first by those who had escaped the draft and then by returnees.

"I can give you your old job back, and at the same salary, but I can't promise you what it'll be like in a couple of weeks or a month from now." His old boss was sounding like he was doing Howie a favor. "We certainly want to do the best we can for our returning service men," he added, "but it's really dog-eat-dog out there right now, and things are rough."

Howie's first day back was worse than the front line at Pont-a-Mousson. By the time he was back on 105th Street, stumbling up the steps of the Boulding apartment building, he was in the depths of despair. How could he find work, find a home and support his family? The best he could do was arrange with Dad Andrews to stay with him in Philadelphia and come in every morning in search of a new job—one that would support his new family—and find an apartment that would house all three, one that he could afford. The welcome-home to the men who had served their country may have been genuine, but the amenities that went with it were far from sufficient.

Chapter Twenty

"Oh, I've been desperate to find you," Nana gushed. "There was a phone call, and I had no way of finding you. I called the *Sun*, but they didn't even know who you are, and then . . . . "

Howie cut her off. "Who was it?"

"A man by the name of Ken Hall. He said he knew you back in . . . "

"Where is he? Did he leave a number? Is he here in New York?"

Apsley mercifully cut in calmly, "He's here in New York, and he's staying at a hotel down in the financial district. The number's on that pad over on the phone table."

Howie lunged for the phone table, dialed the number and was talking to Ken before Nana could add a word. Ken's voice was the most welcomed, soothing sound he'd heard since leaving Springfield.

"How are you, old buddy? Back banging a typewriter for the *Sun*? Where are you living? Boy, you're lucky to find a place in New York, now. Right?"

Howie picked his way through the conversation carefully, like treading on an ant hill—more factual than poetic, considering his Aunt Nana standing a few feet away, mouth open, gaping in anticipation of whatever news the call would bring.

"Well, the fact is, Ken, the old *Sun* job just isn't there any more. I spent the day rummaging around, looking for something I could do, but the paper is just chock full of guys they picked up during the war plus those who came back before I did. I don't even have a place to stay. Living out in Philly with my dad. I'm just here on the Island looking for a place to get settled."

"Well, looks like you and I found each other at the right time. I'm down here as the new Advertizing Manager for The National Bank of Commerce, and I'm looking for men to set up their new Liberty Loan Committees. You'd be perfect."

Howie was too stunned to respond.

"You still there, Howie?"

"Yes. Oh, my God."

"Well, salary's not bad. $35 to $40 a week. Should double in a couple of years. The only catch is that you'd have to work out on Staten Island. That's where you'd set up the whole system."

"Oh, gaud, Ken, you're a life saver."

"Well, Staten Island's not heaven, but it's a lot more like Suffield than Manhattan is." He laughed. Howie couldn't help joining in. Nana poked him in the ribs.

"What's so funny? You all right?" she asked.

Howie put his hand over the mouthpiece and whispered to her, "I've got a job. We're saved." Then he uncovered the mouthpiece and belted, "When would I start?"

"Well, if you get down here first thing in the morning I can put you on salary starting tomorrow."

That was all Howie needed to know. The rest of the conversation was taken up with directions how to find the National Bank of

Commerce and what to wear and, of course, what to say when they appeared before the big shots.

Once the conversation ended, Howie turned to Apsley to explain. "The bank Ken is with is starting a new program called Savings Accounts. Apparently the Federal Government is encouraging people to start saving money to build up the economy. They're asking banks to have people put money into these Savings Accounts—they'll be different from Checking Accounts—more stable—and banks will use that money to lend to businesses just starting up or expanding and then pay the Savings Accounts some of the interest earned. Everybody shares and everybody gets rich." He glowed with enthusiasm, clapped hands like a little boy and all but leaped and clicked his heels.

Apsley knit his brows, nodded his head and added, "Sort of like investing in the stock market."

"Yes, but in smaller amounts and a lot more investors. And! A lot less trouble and fuss. Everybody wins."

"And the folks in Washington thought this up?"

"That's the way Ken explained it. Or, at least they're behind it and pushing it with all sorts of tax breaks and so forth. Hey, this country's on a toboggan ride. We're headed for big time. By 1930 we'll all be millionaires."

Chapter Twenty One

Howard Andrews' prediction of "millionaires by 1930" was accompanied by other ironies in his philosophy and his behavior. Nevertheless, he successfully transported his family of two from rural Massachusetts to rural Staten Island where they lived in a dark, muddy brown, wooden house which they called "the dirty house." There Ellie set about to clean it and set up housekeeping while Howie journeyed by ferry to Wall Street daily to join Ken Hall in setting up headquarters for the Savings Deposit system bent on convincing the banking world that money lent was money well spent.

And it worked. In a few years Howie had made contact with every bank on Staten Island and even oversaw the creation of Savings and Loan institutions that encouraged workers and housewives to "put a little something away," thereby creating numerous funds available for entrepreneurs and their new industries, new enterprises, new jobs available. That part of Howie's prediction was charging full speed ahead, and in short order life on the Island in the Harbor became far more sophisticated than it had been or might even conceivably have been for a Hell's Kitchen offspring whose family had deserted him—through unnatural as well as natural causes.

But Howard never felt that circumstances which threw him into his "abandoned" state had ironically fed his natural talents with the energy and determination so helpful for success. Instead, he kept a begrudging nature despite life's considerable rewards. Still, he was riding high, riding to work each day on the Staten Island train that ran from Tottenville at the southern tip of Staten Island, where General Washington once had his headquarters, all along the East coast to St. George where the Manhattan and Brooklyn ferries docked. From there the ferry took him to New York for just a quarter and, once there, he had only to make his way to the office with a healthy walk or a short subway ride. But, there he was safely ensconced in a good job, a successful and innovative program and a life style befitting a man with talent, good sense and a hero's record as a veteran of "The War to End All Wars." What more could he ask for? Now all he had to do was bring that same ingenuity and discipline to his domestic life.

Ellie was also all he could ask for—and more. Gentle, pliant, always concerned about details, a good housewife, housekeeper, home maker, not the most exciting person to share life with, but certainly unsurpassable in loyalty and responsibility.

But they needed a new house—one of his own design, not like "the dirty house"—and the piece of property down the line in Great Kills was just the answer. A little inovatively due to the cost of such an operation, he first built the left half, the half with the kitchen, living room and, upstairs bedrooms and bath. Then, as finances allowed, he attached the right half with the dining and breakfast rooms downstairs and the master bedroom and dressing room upstairs. It worked beautifully, even if the tug on the left half cracked the back wall of the living room. That was taken care of with an upright piano covering the blemish. Besides, there was always plaster and fresh wallpaper to come.

Yes, he had the answer to everything, and his wartime mantra of responsibility and command was taking shape in the household as it had in the army and now in his job.

Twin beds may have been a cumbersome manifestation of his painstakingly acquired social status, but Howie made the trip from one to the other nevertheless, sufficiently to bring forth his second male heir, this one named in recognition of and gratitude to Ken Hall.

The bed hopping turned out to be more bothersome than adventurous, and pregnancy was certainly no help. The girls who cruised up and down Wall Street environs began to look more and more interesting, but he clung to the sacredness of his vows and examined streetwalkers only from a distance. He got his titillation from others in the office who whispered tales of escapades when they gathered in the men's room. Howard had taken his vows, and he honored them.

Young Kenneth, Ken Hall's namesake, arrived just at the time when the Andrews household moved to the new house—or at least the first half of it—on Nelson Avenue in Great Kills. The new baby and his four-year-old brother kept Ellie hopping, but the neighbors were not denied or disappointed when they came to call. After all, they'd been through all that themselves, and new homes, new children and new neighbors were blossoms to a bee. Thus, the Andrews' first contacts in Great Kills were via the Women's Club and, then, the Bridge Club. Social life may have been a little less than what Howie had anticipated, but it was flattering and certainly just the ticket for Ellie and her two offspring. Howie even found himself back in uniform making a speech in the Public School 8 schoolyard on Armistice Day, an honor preserved by news photographers.

"Don't you think he's turning a little blue?" Ellie shifted the nursing chore from left to right while Howie oversaw the maneuver with a subtle combination of pride and eroticism.

"You mean Kenneth? He looks all right to me."

"I'm going to ask the doctor tomorrow. He has a checkup. I don't like the way he looks."

Dr. Caughlin showed up at 10:30 the next morning, parking his car in the stump of a roadway intended to eventually cut through the woods and connect Nelson Avenue with Cleveland Avenue which, half a mile away, ran through the middle of the woods between the two streets. He ambled his bulky weight along Nelson Avenue and up the steps to the front walk and then tapped the knocker several times. Ellie was ready for him and ushered him into the living room where she nervously poured out her concerns.

Dr. Caughlin examined baby Kenneth quickly and then took a long look at Ellie, his eyes wandering down over her slight but swollen frame. Then he opened his doctor's kit and took out the stethoscope, pulled Ellie over to a chair where he sat down and began running the scopic part over the front of her dress. In a moment he stopped, looked up at her, and said quietly, "No wonder he's turning blue. You're starving him. I have a feeling you're pregnant with his little brother—or sister."

Ellie had to sit down.

He looked at her with a wry twinkle. "You haven't been taking time out, have you?" She didn't respond readily, and he went on gently, "Well, I can understand the difficulty in this sort of forbearance, but you might have refrained for just a bit longer. At least till we see what the Lord has in store for us. I think it would be wise if you come in to the office and let me give you a more thorough examination."

Billie arrived just sixteen months after the birth of his brother, Ken. He was a scrawny little urchin, all wiggles and giggles and requiring more than just double the baby care Ellie had been accustomed to. Kenneth quickly moved on to the bottle.

Howie adapted less easily to his boys than he did to his garden. A garden was a place where he could actually get involved—

personally, get his hands on things, make them grow, grow the way they should, with guaranteed results. His garden was a considerable achievement for a boy raised on cement sidewalks. He liked tillng the soil, planting the vegetables and weeding the rows. And he didn't have to waste time seeing if they understood or had any complaints or approved of having a garden in the first place. Plant a plant, and that's all there is to it. Plant it, and it stays planted.

First there were the rhubarb plants. Then rows of squash, carrots, beans, potatoes and onions followed by lattice-work festooned with tomatoes and then, bringing up the rear, tall stalks of corn. The garden stretched from his back yard all the way across the property behind his neighbor Mr. Stone's house, property he had bought just so he could cultivate such a garden, create for himself—and family—a dominion running behind all the houses on that side of Nelson Avenue.

In addition, Howie erected poles and crossbeams for a grape arbor that masked the Stone's house both at the side and the back. In a few short years they were festooned with huge clusters of grapes, blue and green. It was only a short step from there to the brewing of home-made wine. Elie never mentioned her concerns over alcohol, because there was a certain elegance to wine. Howie made sure of that with a beautiful hand painted wine decanter with which he filled their glasses, and the elegant ritual of toasts which preceded each meal. Wine, like the champagne of their wedding night, was not alcohol. It was elegance.

Howie smiled at her from the opposite end of the long diningroom table, delicate wine glass elevated. "To you," he intoned dramatically.

"To us," she answered as the boys stared, mouths agape, at their parents' antics.

Howie was eager to step up and out with style. Wine became his initial in-house, domestic plant, dinner with wine, a toast to his beautiful bride under the watchful eyes of his ogling offspring. Then something else entered the household. Another sign of prestige, perhaps, but one that thrilled one and all. And that was a dog. Not a little runt or some conglomeration of mutt with no ancestry, but a full pedigreed breed with class. Howard settled on a Police Dog and then labored over the choice between German Shepherd or Belgian. The Belgians were prettier, and, besides, the kennel he surveyed had a host of beautiful beasts.

His first choice was a cute little pup he called "Whiskey and Soda." "Soda" for short. Another tickle at the Massachusetts sobriety fix to accompany his own developing expertise as a vintner. But, sadly, Soda didn't last long. Howard thought it was distemper, but Ellie knew it was overfeeding—being stuffed, actually—on the part of the three ebullient boys. That plus bodies of the deceased beasts found down in the dingle.

Back Howie went to the kennels, and this time he returned with a handsome pup, all black on top with brown legs and underbelly. This one would reflect the majesty that belonged to a Belgian Shepherd. He was named "Thor" for the Nordic God of Thunder. And he was also taught not to eat without first gaining permission, a precaution against garbage and dead animals. The large bowl of dog food was denied him with shouts of "No, no!" plus a few whacks on the snout with a rolled up newspaper until the master deemed enough time had passed to ensure Thor's total submission. Then the master would yell gleefully, "OK, TAKE IT!," and the ravenous pooch would gleefully pounce on the dog dish and devour his daily ration like a Hoover vacuum cleaner.

"That'll keep him from eating the neighbor's garbage and dead animals he finds in the dingle," Howard explained.

The next step was a whip, a legitimate instrument of discipline and training purchased at the pet shop. Howard learned to crack it along side Thor when the dog dish was set out and once or twice even laid across the animal's back if he lunged for his sustenance. Whatever the timing and whatever the method, Howard and his whip ultimately developed complete mastery over his pet and disciple, the ever adoring and ever obedient Thor.

The family took note

At the same time, Howie took note of his situation—kinda' like an "Equipment Check" in the Army . . . Position, Personal and Equipment."

Position: a house of his own design, garden, gold fish pond and all. Not bad.

Personal: a wife, three kids, a dog. Not bad.

Equipment: a job, two assistants, money flowing. Not bad., not bad. Not bad at all.

"A millionaire down the road," he thought. "Maybe not a millionaire," he mulled, "but darn close, maybe."

Chapter Twenty Two

The 1920s, known in Manhattan for its razz-ma-tazz, produced more military autocracy in the Andrews household—military management, military instruction, military rules. The dog whip was in play even with one of the two-legged disciples when a report card arrived with an unacceptable F for deportment. There seemed to be a lot of rebellion once the two youngest were let loose on the school grounds. Not with Howard Junior, for, as the eldest, he had learned quickly that the two most important rules of the Andrews household—important but unspoken—were "obey quickly" and "keep your mouth shut." In time, his two younger siblings dubbed him, "The Clam."

But as discipline and organization developed strength and importance within the household, politics and the business world were staggering and tripping over each other. Howard's prediction of "Millionaires by 1930" was being drowned along with a submerging Stock Market. His whip-cracking beneficence did not stretch as far as Wall Street, and as the Stock Market slid so did the efforts of the Liberty Loan Committee and Ken Hall's own National Bank of

Commerce. Howard's visits to factory superintendents persuading them that, for the industrial good, "employees should spend sensibly and save wisely" were tapering off. More than that, the workers themselves had made it clear that after spending sensibly there was little to save wisely. Superintendents did not welcome Howard either sensibly or wisely, and his two "secretaries" who had been busy scooping up the proceeds for the Bank of Commerce were soon to leave the service.

Command Responsibility was taking a blow. Howard and Ellie sat in their lawn chairs by the gold fish pond he had labored to build, close to the vegetable garden and grape arbors he had created, the patient and all subservient but loving Thor at his side, ears flicking forward and back as his master graced him with attention and affection.

"You know, Ellie, I never know when I go in each morning if I'm going to do my job or start sweeping the hallways." He paused, but she didn't say a word. "Even my two girls are already gone."

"What two girls?"

"My two secretaries, the ones who follow up with each factory or business making out the reports on how the savings program is going."

"Oh, I didn't know. About them, I mean."

Howard scowled. How could she not know about the girls? I've talked about what I do there for almost a decade, now, he thought. Nobody gives a rap about what I have to do to support this family.

"We're pulling out in about a week."

"You're leaving? Why?" Howie sank into the guest chair in Ken Hall's office all but aglaze over the news.

"You know the situation here," Ken went on. "It's deteriorating in a way none of us expected. I don't have to tell you, Howie. The staff has been decimated. Even your two assistants are gone.

We're just not generating enough investments for the bank to justify support for the program—and the staff that goes with it. And that means us." Ken paused a bit, looking around the office room, comfortable, well organized, well appointed—deceiving. "Swept out, I might even say."

Howard watched. "We're all going, aren't we?" Howard asked.

Ken's gaze snapped back onto his. "Yes—eventually." Silence again took over.

"What are you going to do back in Massachusetts?"

"Well, the old bank's still there, and some of the old guys are retiring. They've offered one of those slots for me since they've known me so long. And Polly. And the war, of course." He paused again, looking squarely at Howard.

"But you've got opportunities I don't have," he continued. "Talents. I got you on board because you can do things, special things like promote. There's still a business world out there. You have contacts. Don't you?" he asked after a beat.

Howie thought of those he'd worked with at the Sun. A couple of them had gone into advertising. He wished he'd stayed in touch. He kept silent.

"I've got a couple of contacts I can connect you with," Ken broke in.

Howie couldn't help but grin. Back to the post war debacle. No job, no future. Once again Ken to the rescue. At least this time he had a house. And a family, he couldn't help but note. But then he added a mental tag—both have to be paid for. He dug his chin into his chest and mumbled, "Damn Germans."

Ken's head jerked a bit, and a slight smile crossed his face as he asked, "Why the Germans?"

Howie spit the answer back. "They should have paid those Reparations for The World War years ago. Now here it is, 1929, and they're just agreeing to pay up for all the damage they did. And they're in better shape than we are. What's this fellow's name?

Hitler? He ought to pay that money to us so we can get on with building America, make up for all the Huns cost us to stop the Kaiser and save Europe." His eyes glared.

Ken stared back, a half grin creeping across his face. "Winning a war doesn't mean you don't have to pay for it." The two sat silently, Howie glaring back, seeking to find the logic in that statement. Finally, he spoke.

"Well, those Reparations have to go somewhere, and we need the money. After all, we won the damn war for them. They owe us something."

Ken answered. "They owe us eternal gratitude plus the expectation we'll step in and save them any time they need us." And he paused. "Or any time we feel someone needs saving." Again nothing was said for several minutes. Then Ken grinned and shifted in his chair. "By the way, when you said those Reparations ought to go to 'us,' who did you mean by 'us?'"

"I meant 'us,' the people who need it," Howie snapped.

"Give it to the Liberty Loan program?" Ken's grin grew broader. "Or maybe dump it on Wall Street, on the Stock Market. Use it to buy stock in America. Let Germany buy American stock, American industry, buy up all American business." He paused, eyeing Howie as his grin grew and grew. "Welcome Germany, the new owners of American business."

Howie couldn't help but finally grin, himself. "Ken, don't be a smart ass."

Ken nodded, smiled broadly and added, "Of course not. The only way America can pull out of this Depression is by pulling itself out."

"Sell more apples on the street."

"No, selling more apples to Germany. For my money, these Reparations are a mistake, like kicking a fellow when he's down. We should be building up the German economy so they'd buy more of our apples, and our Fords and our Hups and those trucks and stuff we use to make roads. We need to sell—sell—sell! Build more, sell more! That's how we're going to get ourselves out of this Depression"

Howie couldn't help but grin. Silently, he stared at Ken. Then he asked, still grinning, "What are you, a Socialist?"

"No, I'm a Republican, just like you—and the rest of New England. Don't forget where the President comes from—Plymouth, Vermont. And you know what he says."

Howie mumbled sarcastically, "Old Silent Cal."

Ken snapped back, "That's right, but when Coolidge speaks it makes sense: *The business of America is business.* Don't you forget that."

Howie mumbled again. "Apples to Germany?"

"Apples anywhere," Ken popped back. "We need to wake this country up, take responsibility for what we're facing, for what we have and what we've done, make the word *business* mean something. You said it yourself, this country needs to feed itself. That's the only way we'll get out of this Depression."

"Now you're sounding like a Democrat."

"Well, when the Democratic Party wakes up, I may switch."

Howie grinned at Ken. He'd never seen him so worked up before. Still grinning, he threw him a barb, "That or have another war."

Ken was clearly startled by this. "How the hell can you say that?"

"Well, when this guy Hitler—or Schickelgruber, or whatever his name is—gets through taking over Europe we'll have plenty of cause to step in and tell them how to run things, except that this time we'll set up not just Democracy, but we'll set up the markets as well."

Ken shook his head slowly, "You know, Howie, sometimes I worry about you."

"Mark my words, Ken. We're going to have another war, and this time we're going to build 'business' into the winning." The two of them paused once again, and Howie placed a tag on his final comment: "Mark my words."

There was silence for several moments. Again, Howie spoke, very quietly. "We're all going, aren't we?"

"To war?"

"No, back to Massachusetts."

"Well, I am. I don't know about you, but Polly and I are."

"Are you driving up?"

"Hell, I don't own a car. Having a car in Manhattan is like roller skating up to the Third Avenue El."

Howie grinned.

"We'll wait till the movers move out and then take a cab to Grand Central Station and the New Haven Railway home. Back to home. Where things are peaceful and we can enjoy the countryside filled with tent-tobacco. Maybe then I'll buy a car."

Howie kept quiet about Ken and Polly's departure until the time they were packed up and leaving the luxury of East Side Manhattan. Ellie was stunned. She was sensitive to the fact that living on separate islands even in the New York harbor had resulted in very few visits from old CLI friends—but, this? Pulling up stakes and going back home?

Back in the New York office, it was one of those mornings when Howie didn't know whether he was to sign up candidates for Liberty Loan or sweep the halls. He went from one desk drawer to another trying to remember where he'd put "that damned note" he'd written a month ago about the bank in Tottenville. Fussing and fuming, he didn't notice his friend from down the hall now standing in front of his desk making little "hey, notice me" noises.

Howie stopped foraging and looked up, staring blankly for a second or two. Then his coworker spoke.

"There's a jigaboo in the outer office asking about you."

"A what?" Howie almost blasted him.

"You know. A negra, a black guy."

"You mean "a Negro?"

"Yeah. Says you knew him. Name's Al-bare Boo-Droo—or something like that."

Howie knew exactly who he meant. "Boudreau," he mumbled. "Sergeant Boudreau! Or Lieutenant Boudreau, he corrected himself. Never knew his first name. "Albert," giving it the French—or Haitian pronunciation—"Albair."

Howie's visitor obviously didn't intend that the announcement was going to be so convoluted—or take this long. "What do you want me . . . . ?

Howie bolted from his seat, skirted both the desk and his visitor and raced down the hall. When he got to the outer lobby, there he was. Boudreau was spiffy in a Fifth Avenue suit, classy tie and a grin from ear to ear.

The two just stared at each other, Boudreau grinning and Howie mouth agape. Finally, Howie found his tongue.

"Boudreau," he blurted, shaking the man's hand. "My God, how long's it been?"

"Just a war or two," grinned Boudreau.

Howie finally gathered his wits and burbled, "Come on in. For God's sake, come on down to my office. My God, what a surprise. I mean, to see you." He finally gave up on the small talk and, taking the Sergeant—or the Lieutenant—or the man—the Black Man, that is—left a gaping receptionist and headed back down the hall to his office. On the way he passed the gaping messenger of Boudreau's arrival, flattening himself against the wall and watching the odd couple whisking by.

Once Howie got a chair pulled up along side the desk—not in front of, but aside—he sat down, swivelled himself around to face Boudreau and did his best to calm down.

"Well—what have you been up to? Not since Hell's Kitchen and the Cadillac Hotel, of course, but at least sine the war."

Boudreau couldn't stifle a smile. Calm and self contained, he slowly crossed a leg, leaned back and grinned. "Well, I couldn't go back to being a pearl-diver or a bus boy, so I decided to be a business man. I figured I'd had enough training for that while in the Army. Remember? 'Officer and a Gentleman,' I believe it was we were called. Right?"

Howie couldn't help but match him, grin for grin.

"Well, one thing led to another, and it became clear that Negroes like myself don't really have anything or anyone to speak for them. No books, no magazines, and only a few rags of newspapers you can pick up on the street, and, even then, rare and hard to find, to say nothing of being off on some cloud and lousy reading."

Howie became aware that he was sitting there with his mouth wide open, staring at this new incarnation of the dish washer, platoon sergeant, army officer, snappy dressed New Yorker talking with him like some big business executive. It took a bit of doing to digest all that at one sitting.

Boudreau stopped for a moment, obviously aware that he'd been going on and on with not a scintilla of reaction from his ex-Platoon Leader. The silence only invited him to go on.

"And so I started a magazine—for Negroes—or Blacks, as we're being called. And beginning to call ourselves, I might add. I call the magazine *Noir*, which I guess you can figure out with your high school French."

Howie chuckled. "I'd forgotten you were Haitian. You think everybody'll get it?"

"Well, if not, they'll pick up a copy if they're curious, and we'll have a cross-culture dialogue."

"So, you hope to sell to both blacks and whites?"

"Yes, and there's where you come in. Why I'm here."

Howie stiffened, imperceptibly, he hoped.

"I want this magazine to have some class and some knowhow. I remember you'd worked for the Sun, so I knew you knew the newspaper world—knew about communication, selling, image, that sort of thing." He paused a bit. "I need somebody who can offer the reader a service but, at the same time, sell himself—or, in this case, us."

There was a long pause. Things had taken a direction Howie could not have imagined, one that obviously Boudreau knew they would, so Howie knew he couldn't push. He waited. Finally, he spoke.

"How'd you find me?"

Boudreau grinned. "Serendipity, you might say. I was actually getting together in a sort of Negro Officer's Society when I ran across some from the old outfit, the 351st from the 92nd Division. Your name came up, and I thought it'd be neat to track you down. It wasn't difficult. I headed for the newspaper—the Sun, first, and folks up there knew where you were. You may be a bit more well known than you think. Anyway, I found you about the time I was launching *Noir*, and it was clear that running into you might have been fate's way of responding to my needs."

Howie stammered a bit but managed to ask, "How would you want me to . . . . I mean, how would I . . . . ?"

Boudreau smiled. "I want you to work for *Noir*. Full time." He paused a bit, the smile still there. "Not up in Harlem where we'll be printing, but somewhere over on the East Side. I've been scouting offices, and there's a nice place we can handle just east of the Village, and I'll set you up there. You can work alone, or, if things go the way I think they will, you can select your own staff and you're in business—Promotion, Advertising, P.R. for *Noir Magazine*." Boudreau took a deep breath and sat back, waiting. The look on his face made clear that he knew what he was asking—of a white man, as well as one who had once been his superior officer in the Army. He waited.

Howie thought of his conversation with Ken. He thought of the one by the pool with Ellie, with Thor lying beside him, the garden, the grape arbors, the house he had labored to build—and pay for.

"What about salary?"

"I don't know. We'll have to hammer that out—between us. I've talked to the business end of *Noir*, and they know what I'm looking for, what is needed." Again, he paused. "Howie, this magazine has to cross lines or we're not going to succeed—to go where I want it to go. And it will. I'll make sure of that."

"Let me talk with Ellie and get back with you."

"That's fair." Boudreau stood up.

Howie rose slowly, took a step toward the tall, black man, and stuck out his hand. The two clasped hands, warm, confident, encouraging.

Both smiled.

Chapter Twenty Three

Ellie rose up out of the bed and a deep, deep sleep simultaneously. The darkened room all but slammed her back onto the sheets as she flayed her arms to keep from rolling onto the floor. Then silence. She lay motionless, panting, eyes darting from window to window, picking out shards of light and strange shapes.

There it was again! Anger! Anguish! A cry. A moan. She froze, propped up on one elbow, staring at Howie's form in the other twin bed, twisted, mouth agape. They were staring at each other.

"Howard, are you all right?"

The pause was long, almost too long.

"I must have been dreaming," his answer came.

"You scared me to death."

Off in the distance a child's voice half floated, half bounced into the bedroom.

"Mother!"

Ellie turned to the door, calling, "It's all right, dear. We just . . . " She stopped, frozen still for a moment and then whipped the covers off and scurried out of bed, into the hallway and down to the children's bedroom. "You've just had a bad dream . . . ," her voice trailing into the sound of wind whipping around the house.

Howie didn't move. Propped up on one elbow, he turned his head, scanning each of the windows. Slowly, he lowered himself back down, eyes held open as with sticks, hearing again, seeing again the chaos that had invaded his sleep with its senseless nightmare.

Ellie's slippered tip-toes gently turned him as she came to his side and knelt with her hands reaching out for his.

"You were dreaming."

"A God awful nightmare."

She wanted to ask what it had been, but her mind had already skipped through the catalogue of worries he had voiced month after month. Instead, she took his hand and pressed it to her cheek, turning to kiss it over and over and over again.

Hours later, Ellie was serving her husband's cereal and toast when Howard Junior slipped quietly into the breakfast nook. His father looked up, stared at his son and then turned quizzically to Ellie as she brought a third bowl of oatmeal in from the kitchen.

"Howard Junior's starting high school this morning. He has to get up early to take the bus to Tottenville from now on. You know that's the only high school on all the island." She waited briefly, expecting a response, but then went on. "So we'll be having breakfast together. Just the three of us." She smiled at Howard Junior. "Would you like some eggs and toast?"

"No, thanks. The oatmeal will be just fine."

Breakfast was quiet, wordless. Howie kept glancing over at his son and then at Ellie as she buzzed around the breakfast room, back and forth in and out of the kitchen. She looked over at Howard Junior.

"Want some coffee?"

"No, thanks. I'd rather have the milk, if it's OK. Do you have any jelly?"

Ellie took the top from the jelly dish and handed the bowl to him. She smiled as he lathered the toast and crammed half a slice into his mouth, and she turned to Howie, almost laughing, as he stared at his son, sharing breakfast, all but fully grown, not a boy but a man. Ellie could feel the amazement and touch of pride almost glowing from Howie's look of surprise. It was as though he had never really looked at the boy before. And she thought to herself, perhaps he hadn't.

Howie turned to her again, and she was waiting for him. She smiled. He did the same. Almost. Then, without changing the look on his face, Howie said quietly, "Hitler burned the Reichstag last night. I heard it on the radio. The little one in the dressing room. They burned it down."

Ellie smiled. "You mean they burned down the Reichstag, not the radio."

"For God's sake," shouted Howie, "can I open my mouth without your correcting me!"

Howard Junior's eyes snapped onto his father, hunched over his plate, fork in hand, cold fury on his face. The boy looked at his mother, her eyes down, motionless. The picture froze till Ellie rose quietly and took her plate to the kitchen. Howard Junior said nothing while his father returned to devouring his breakfast.

Once his plate was clear, Howie drained his final cup of coffee, rose wordlessly, and moved to the hall closet for his hat and exited the front door with a loud, resounding bang.

Howard Junior had sat, motionless staring at the door through which his father had disappeared, wordless, listening to the sound of doors, opening, closing and, finally, slamming as he visualized his father exiting the house he had, himself, built for his family, wife and children.

Howard Junior rose quietly, slowly, picked up his plate, his cereal bowl, and moved around the breakfast table to the kitchen door. His mother was standing quietly by the stove. She poked the lid handle into one stove top after another, lifting it to check the coals. She moved slowly, almost mechanically.

"Why do you let him talk to you like that?"

Ellie whipped around, startled. "My goodness. I didn't see you there. You scared half the life out of me."

"He talks to you like you were some kind of shop keeper. Worse. Like a trash collector."

"Now, Howard, you shouldn't say such things about your father. He puts the meal on your table, the roof over your head. Besides, he's your father. Show respect."

"Why? He doesn't respect you."

Ellie's jaw dropped. Howard watched her carefully place the stove lid holder in the rack almost automatically, wiping her hands on her apron as she glanced over his shoulder and moved to where he stood at the breakfast room entry. She looked at him and then back to the other door, the one to the living room, before settling herself.

"Howard, you wouldn't have all those things, the nice clothes—your new corduroys, that cap you got last Christmas—if it weren't for the hard work your father takes on every day of the week."

"Yes, and the dog-whipping Billie got for an "F" on his report card."

"Now, that's enough."

"Howard's right," said another voice.

Ellie whipped around to find Kenneth standing in the living room doorway. "I don't know why you put up with the way he speaks to you, the way he treats you." He moved into the kitchen as he spoke. She was now flanked on both sides by the two boys, trapped by the fruit of her loins and words she knew couldn't be argued against.

"Now, hush!"

The three stood silently till it became apparent that tears were ebbing from Mother's eyes, and the apron was losing its battle.

Howard Junior slid his arm around her shoulders. He was as tall as she. They both sensed it for the first time. Kenneth gently touched her elbow and kissed it.

Ellie quickly wrapped her arms about the shoulders of both her oldest boys and kissed their foreheads. She smiled at them. "You're why it's all right." She kissed their foreheads again, gently pushed them away and stood, cheeks moist, smiling at them without saying a word.

"Is breakfast ready?" Billie's voice came crashing through the living room door before his form was propelled into the kitchen. Faced with his mother and two older brothers holding each other at arm's length, he halted, speechless and perplexed. It seemed minutes before anyone said anything.

Howard Junior finally stepped up to the plate. "Your mother was telling us how fortunate the Andrews family is to have three discerning, caring, and productive offspring."

With the exception of Kenneth's quick and quickly suppressed glance at his older brother, the trio didn't move. Billie looked at each of them, especially his mother who was busy examining the linoleum floor. Finally, he said quietly to all, "I think you got a screw loose."

Chapter Twenty Four

It was a household that bespoke the admonition, "Do what you're told and no backtalk." Although never articulated in such strong language, the message came through in everything heard or seen. The family readily obeyed, providing the surest measure of security and privacy.

What was lacking was any degree of camaraderie that normally would link father and sons. Ironically, Howard Junior saw father and son comradery all around him. His bedroom window was only a matter of feet from the neighbors' master bedroom, and every Sunday he would hear little Pete storm into his parents' bedroom, shrieking and giggling as he leaped on their bed, yelling "Hey, Pop!" and wrestling with his dad.

The giggling, the shrieking were nothing but pure joy compared to the imposed silence on the Andrews household, silence demanded until the Pater Familia was up and involved in his morning ablutions.

Sunday was mostly a gardening day, but the three boys, joined tightly in Howard Junior's grip, made their way through the dingle behind the house over to Cleveland Avenue and then up the dirt street to Reverend Minert's Moravian Church for Sunday School. When the parents deigned to attend, their route was more civilized, down Nelson Avenue and then over to the Church on a cross street. It was a family church, but not all the family maintained much of an attendance record.

Howard Junior often wondered about the disparity in and of his family. Where in hell had they all come from? Whose genes did they inherit? Certainly not the same ones he'd been given. Their genes were nothing like his mother's or his father's—thank heaven for the latter. Certainly they could have used a bucket full of the Alderson genes. He couldn't help but chuckle at that thought, although Howard Junior's "chuckles" were really no more than a slight upturn at the corner of the mouth. Which side may have varied, but the degree of lift seldom did.

A stranger in a strange land. That was Howard Junior's fate, he surmised. But why did they have to be so fractious? Kenneth and Billie always scrapping, his father so stand-offish? Well, at least he could play football, hang around his own crowd, be with people that weren't fussin' all the time. Once he got out of the house, he could pick and choose. That's the way life oughta' be.

"Oh, Howard, you're home. How was football practice today?"

Howard let the back porch screen door swing to with a slam/bang and headed on through the kitchen for the front stairs and a shower plus dinner clothes, a jacket and tie. Always a jacket and tie.

"When you get cleaned up, I need to talk with you."

Howard halted in the living room door and stared back at his mother. "What for?"

"Oh, nothing. I just had a wonderful idea for your father and wanted you children to do something."

There was an uncomfortable pause while Howard stood frozen in the doorway and his mother busied herself with the pots and pans, preparing dinner. The clock kept ticking while Howard stared.

"Like what?"

Ellie put down the stirring spoon and returned the lid to the kettle bubbling on the coal stove. She smiled at Howard and wiped her hands on the apron as she came around to where she could see him.

"Yesterday's sermon was a wonderful one about family and the children and parents—everything we all care about. I just wish that the Sunday School classes could have been brought up to the sanctuary so we all could have heard it—together."

Howard was unprepared for this to be a topic of discussion, to say the least. He tried not to look too quizzical as he moved back into the kitchen. "What'd he say?"

"Well, it was about respect—and things we can do to show each other how much we appreciate all that's being done—every day of our lives. Like when you children do the dishes for me every night, with you scraping and stacking for me while Kenneth wipes the breakables and Billie the unbreakables. That tells me you like the dinner and that you thank me—and so on."

There was a pause, a bit awkward for Howard who didn't quite know what direction the conversation was heading. And then it came.

"I got the idea—maybe it was something that Reverend Minert was saying about the Head of the Household—when I got the idea that we never "stack and dry the dishes," you might say, for your father. I got the idea, wouldn't it be great—and great fun—if we were all at the front door when he came home from work so we could say 'welcome home' to him and, in a way, thank him for making everything possible—the dinner, the clothes, and even this house. What do you think?"

There was little Howard Junior could say—or think of, for that matter. He considered that maybe a rehearsal would help. There'd have to be a way to insure that the two brats didn't mess things up. His mother thought that was a great idea, and they agreed to call the two young ones in for a rehearsal.

After Howard Junior's shower there was just enough time for all four to get lined up in the front hall, wearing their jackets and ties, and practice calling out, "Hi, Daddy, welcome home." They ran through that several times while Billie was stationed at the living room window and practiced racing back to formation in the hall whispering loudly, "He's coming up the walk."

Finally the moment came. Precisely as anticipated, the Staten Island train had deposited its cargo, and the Pater Familia had concluded his long trudge up Nelson Avenue to number 97. Then, as the Pater climbed the steps to the front walk, Billie raced from the living room window to the hall whispering wildly, "He's here, he's here, he's coming," and the line straightened out in preparation for the door to creak open. And it did.

"Welcome home, Daddy. Welcome home!" Exactly as rehearsed.

Howie was a bit startled, to say the least, and it took a bit of time to recover from the shock. "Well," he began slowly, his eyes darting from son to son and finally resting on his proud spouse. "This is quite a welcome." He grinned at her and slowly moved to plant and receive the usual "welcome home" kiss, but just at that moment, Billie decided this was all too formal an occasion.

"Hi, Pop!"

Howie stopped and turned back to his irreverent youngest and simply stared at him.

Ellie stepped in quickly and bent down before Billie, wagging a disapproving finger, admonishing, "*Father* or *Dad*, maybe, but *Pop* is not a very respectful thing to call your father."

That didn't slow Billie down one iota as he grinned back, "That's what Pete Stone next door calls his dad. He calls him *Pop*."

Howie hadn't moved an inch. He stared at his youngest and snapped, "Well, you can go next door and call Pete's father *Pop* all you want to, but it's not anything I'd care for." With that, Howie crossed the hall, tossed his fedora onto the chair and turned back to Ellie, still crouched on the floor before Billie. "It's a helluva way to show respect to someone who puts the roof over your head and the food on the table." With that, he charged up the stairs to ready himself for dinner.

The foursome in the hall moved barely an inch. Ellie slowly rose from her crouched position and moved through the dining room into the breakfast room and on into the kitchen, silent and saddened. Howard Junior stared down at his youngest brother and just shook his head. Kenneth lashed out, hissing, "That was a dumb thing to do. You're so stupid," he added fitfully."

Billie simply opened the front door and raced out onto the lawn and around, down into the dingle. Howard Junior pushed Kenneth out of the way and gently closed the front door. Then he went out to the side porch and sat quietly in the swing, awaiting his mother's call, "Dinner's on the table." Before that could happen the sound of his father's footsteps coming down the stairs stiffened him. He leaned out to where he could see the living room entrance to the porch. The double doors were open, lying flat against the outside wall of the house. He could hear his father move through the living room and hear him call into the kitchen, "Ellie, can you come in here a minute?" Howard Junior pulled back onto the porch swing and waited.

"What is it, dear?"

"Where are the kids?"

They've gone outside. What is it?"

"Come here. Sit down. I've got something to tell you."

Howard Junior could hear them move past the open porch doors over to the front of the house and the sofa that awaited them. There was a long stretch of silence. His father spoke first.

"I told you this banking thing was folding. The Stock Market crash, Ken Hall going on back to Suffield, the staff being let go, all that."

His father's voice was now barely audible, and Howard Junior leaned precipitously toward the doors, afraid that the slightest noise would be heard inside. His father's voice ranged from an almost angry declarative to pure mumbling, but the story that was tumbling out was unmistakable. He was leaving the banking business.

"I've been asked to take over promotion and advertising for a new magazine. It's the kind of thing I know I can do and do well. In one sense, it's a great thing. A couple of things, I have to accept . . . but I can do it."

There was a long pause. Howard Junior moved noiselessly to the end of the swing, straining to hear.

"The magazine is owned by someone I knew in France . . . another Lieutenant."

"Well, that will be wonderful." his mother offered cheerfully.

"Well," his father added tentatively, "you remember the 92nd was all black." He paused.

"Except the officers," Ellie added quizzically.

"We commissioned some in France." Again, a pause. There was an unmistakable quiver of uncertainty in his father's voice. "This is one of them. He'd been my Platoon Sergeant, but they commissioned him."

"Well, that was nice," his mother responded after a slight pause. "If it's somebody you know, somebody you served with, someone you trust, it certainly should be all right. Who knows? You might end up with something that will be a big success, something that you can help make successful."

The conversation trailed off with a word or two making its way out onto the porch and Howard Junior's eager ear. Suddenly, his father's voice broke through the mumble, clear and precise. "Don't tell the children . . . . about the fact that it's black, I mean. I don't want the neighborhood gossiping about Andrews working for a Jigaboo."

There was an edge to his father's voice that made Howard Junior smile. He found himself wondering whom he could tell first. He quickly faced the fact that he wouldn't know what to say if he did. His mental meanderings were broken by his mother's voice, loud and clear.

"What was the name of the magazine, did you say?"

"Noir."

"That's French. It means 'black,' doesn't it?"

"Or 'night time,' or 'dark,' or something like that."

"Isn't that odd."

"Well," his father answered after a slight pause, "it's not half as odd as "Albair" Boudreau himself."

"What do you mean?"

This time the pause seemed like forever. His mother's voice returned, hesitantly. "That was what you were dreaming about the other night, wasn't it?" Then she added, "The nightmare."

There was no answer. It seemed like minutes before Howard Junior could hear someone moving across the room. Then he heard his father at the kitchen door calling back, "Dinner about ready?"

Chapter Twenty Five

The Great Depression took its toll on virtually everyone in the country, and yet Howie managed the cutbacks and terrifying uncertainties by virtue of the security of his position as Advertising and Promotion Coordinator for a negro magazine. Still, while Lieutenant . . . Sergeant . . . pearl diver "Albair" Boudreau may have created a haven in the social storm, he was also partly responsible for that still cankerous resentment fostered by Howard Andrews' Hell's Kitchen upbringing. For Howie it was a precarious balance of gratitude and prejudice.

Boudreau had made things easier for Howie by setting him up in his own office on the east side of Greenwich Village. On his first day with the company, Howie was invited up to the main office in Harlem where he was to be introduced and issued the keys to his East Village office. Ironically, Boudreau was called away on a business deal and was unable to meet him and show him around. Everybody was nice, though, apparently well prepared for the "honkey" on the staff. Howie received his keys and quickly left.

He had made the trip from Battery Park to Harlem via the subway, but this time he took a cab and directed the driver to his East Village office almost all the way down at the foot of Manhattan. The place was the third story of a lunch shop with a photographer's studio occupying the floor in between. He introduced himself to the restaurant owner and then the photographer and continued on up the steps to his own digs. Giving the key a bit of a flourish, he pushed the door open and stood for a moment surveying his new domain. Not bad! Nice desk, chair, guest chair, a large easel, even a lounge for group meetings or perhaps even a cat nap if he wanted. Even better than his old office with the Liberty Loan Committee. What a transition! Born in Hell's Kitchen and now located in Greenwich Village. Better yet, the East Side, the fashionable side, the poff side. Not bad at all.

Slowly, grinning from ear to ear, he sauntered in, gently touched the guest chair, and proceeded on to his own behind the desk. Carefully, slowly, savoring it, he lowered himself into the seat and leaned back. As his eyes scanned upward, it was a shock to see Boudreau standing in the open doorway, grinning, staring at him.

"Welcome to your new home," came the greeting. "You like it?"

Howie returned the grin as he glanced around. "Very much. You did a nice job." He looked back at Boudreau. "Thanks."

The tall, dark man moved into the room, picking up the guest chair as he went and planting it along side of Howie. "And, if you're comfortable with it, let's make it 'Howie' and 'Al.' Does that bother you?"

Howie was struggling so hard to keep up, he didn't quite make it before Boudreau . . . that is, Albert . . . or Al . . . moved on. "It beats 'Al—baire,' doesn't it?"

Again, Howie could only smile—sickly, it seemed. His boss went on. "I've told everyone on the staff we're all on a first name basis. Did they treat you that way up at the main office?" This time the boss waited.

"Yes, they were great." Howie tried not to stutter and stammer. His first visit to the Head Office in Harlem had been quite a challenge, even . . . or, perhaps especially . . . for a Lower West Side boy.

"Sorry I couldn't be there. I had a matter with the printing I had to take care of and couldn't break away. I told them the reason you were Down Town, here, was so you could keep close to the business world and make sure 'Noir' transcended any barriers."

Howie smiled and nodded a bit . . . and then more. This was not his usual office banter, but he realized that it was exactly what had been steeping . . . he didn't want to say "festering" . . . in his own mind. What impressed him was that it was being discussed by Boudreau . . . 'Al,' that is . . . and not himself. The world was changing.

Almost as if he had been reading Howie's mind, Al went on, "Yes, things are changing. I'm not sure why, what kicked it in the ass . . . maybe it was the war; it did somewhat for me . . . but I've been thinking somewhat of those days when I was 'pearl diving' for the Cadillac Hotel and your father was 'Maitre d'." He paused a moment as if for Howie's response, but Howie just stared. He was with the "pearl diver" every step of the way, but he could think of nothing to add. Al went on.

"That day when Diamond Jim Brady visited us, you remember?"

Howie was mute. He nodded his head.

"I said something to you when I climbed down off the famous Brady lap and walked by you on the way back to the kitchen. You remember?"

Again, Howie could only nod.

"I called you 'White Boy.' I suspect it was the same as you calling me "Black Boy" . . . or something worse. Right?"

Howie shifted in his chair. "No, not really. I knew you didn't mean any harm by it."

"But it was a kick in the pants, nevertheless, wasn't it? You knew I was getting back at you, not because I got a quarter and you got boxed in the ear by your father. More like I was black and got a quarter while you were white and didn't. Right?"

Howie eyed the desk top for a second, the space between them.

"I'm here to apologize, Howie." He paused. "I wanted to do that when I was made your Platoon Sergeant and then again when we were fellow Lieutenants." Another pause. "Is it too late?"

Howie looked up. He stared at the man, his fellow veteran, his boss. "Hell, Al, it's I who should be apologizing . . . for two hundred years of slavery and segregation."

Al laughed, unexpectedly. "Now, now, Howie, I'm not going to let you apologize for every "honkey" in America. Hey, you know who brought those slave candidates to the docks in Africa? It wasn't you fellows. You were too chicken to go into the woods and capture us," he went on, chuckling. "Hell, we were captured by our next door neighbors, the tribes down the road. They were the ones who captured my ancestors and took them to the docks."

"And then we paid for them."

"Well, I have to admit you didn't treat us too well, but we did get a trans-Atlantic voyage. No charge."

"And no vacation."

"Or minimum wage." The two were laughing, now. Howie broke in, "People are just no damn good, are they?"

They had their laugh, the banter went on for half an hour, and then they stood and shook hands. It was Howie's turn, now.

"I want to thank you for what you said—all of it. And I'm glad to be here. I hope I can be as good a P.R. for you as you were a Platoon Sergeant for me."

Al smiled. "I'm not worried."

Everything was managed by phone or by runner. Even his paycheck arrived with a grinning teenager who, by the look on his face, certainly must have known the "Boss Boudreau" was protecting his creative "honky" by positioning him in the Village. Howie couldn't help but feel grateful, but he managed to suppress his gratitude by taking the arrangement for granted.

For a while, Howie arrived at Battery Park on the Staten Island ferry and then took the 6th Avenue "El" up to his office, but in a few days he abandoned the ride on the "Elevated" and began walking the distance for both health and curiosity reasons. His appetite and curiosity were more than satisfied. What he liked were especially the girls. As he walked by them or watched them from his office window he wallowed in thoughts of freedom and indulgence for which the Village was known. He felt viscerally that if one of them ever presented herself to him he would leap at the chance like any west side animal should. He often thought back on his last years in Hell's Kitchen and wondered what life would be like if he'd never left "Little Old New York."

At the same time he began to notice changes in Battery Park. For one thing, there cropped up half a dozen recruiting stalls between the 6th Avenue and 3rd Avenue "Els." He watched as young men stopped by and chatted with the sergeants stationed there, ending up with pamphlets which each visitor glanced through while walking away.

The sergeant looked up at Howie, smiled and called out, "Interested?" Howie couldn't tell whether or not there was a touch of facetiousness in his tone, but he was well aware of the difference in their ages.

"I've done my bit," he called back, smiling. "France, in 1918."

The sergeant's expression changed to one of obvious respect. "Oh? What branch?"

Howie smiled and sauntered over. "Artillery. 351st, attached to the 92nd."

The sergeant's face lit up in obvious recognition, and he answered smile for smile, "That must have been an interesting assignment. I take it you were . . . . ?" He paused for a response.

"A lieutenant—Second."

"No gangplank promotion?"

"None." He wondered what the recruiter would say if he told him he was on his way to work for a company that was owned by his former Platoon Sergeant.

The sergeant shuffled through some papers and flyers and added, "But, you know, we still might be able to use you." He paused a bit. "And you still might be able to get that promotion. A couple of them, in fact."

Now he was interested. "What do you mean?" he asked carefully.

"Well, you know there's a whole new branch of service in the Army, now. Same with the Navy and the Marines. It's called the Army Air Corps, and it's big stuff. Lots of openings for officers, Company Grade and Field Grade, both," he added with a sly grin. "A fellow like yourself with officer credentials . . . overseas, especially . . . would probably find lots of openings in the Air Corps . . . non-flying, of course. Sound interesting?"

To Howie it certainly was, but too much so as to allow himself to be led in that direction. "Got anything on paper?" he ventured.

"Just a leaflet and an address in Washington to contact for more data. Here," he added after fishing around in the shelves beneath the booth's counter.

Howie glanced at it. No specifics. More flirtatious than factual. He glanced up at the recruiter. "Mind if I keep this?"

"It's yours," came the answer. "How about giving me your name?"

Howie thought a minute before responding. "Let's put that off till later." He moved quickly from the sergeant's vicinity, stuffing the brochure into his jacket as he increased his pace. It was the first time he'd made his way to the office on foot thinking of the old Army days instead of girls.

Chapter Twenty Six

Crossing the threshold of his third story office in West Greenwich Village was like turning on an electric switch. All was business. All was responsibility. All was . . . . what?

Howie was there for one simple reason . . . . to make *Noir* a successful magazine, a magazine for Blacks to be proud of and for people of all races to be attracted to. He had stood before countless newspaper and magazine stalls all over Manhattan, struggling to determine what made each publication popular. He couldn't help notice that it was the cover which caught the eye. Sure, the departments and sections within made the habitual buyer and subscriber keep coming back, but it was the cover that caught the eye. Each magazine had its own special brand or style of cover, from *Life Magazine* to *Women's Home Companion.*

Howie thought about past issues of *Noir* that he'd scoured since joining the firm. What was the cover saying? What did it promise? What did it guarantee the reader with every issue?

Crossing in front of the restaurant that formed the basis of his office building, he had glanced through the large, plate glass windows to see how many breakfast eaters had been attracted. But he couldn't avoid checking to see if any of the good looking *dolls* were waiting on tables. When he got to the second floor he couldn't help cracking open the door to say "Hi" to his neighbor, the photographer, while he was really checking to see if he had any good looking models this morning. By the time he crossed the threshold of his own office, his mind was cluttered with good looking females of all stripes and allures.

Howie stopped in the middle of the room as though he'd been hit over the head by a rolled up copy of his own magazine. Girls! Of course, that would catch the eye of every male and the judicial stare of every female. But, a picture of girls doing what?

The mirror over the sofa gave back a puzzled look as if to ask, "What are you looking at?" Gradually, purposefully, his mirrored reflection morphed into a pretty young girl combing her luxurious, long, black, hair and asking that very same question. A pretty, young African girl! She stared quizzically and then slowly began to smile at him as if to say, "I know why you're staring at me. It's because you think I'm pretty. You'd like to get to know me better, wouldn't you? Well, just purchase *Noir* and we'll get to know each other just fine. I'll tell you all about myself. And you'll tell me all about you, won't you?"

Howie dashed to the easel and sketched the illusion with the smile of the prettiest dark-skinned female he could imagine. And then he stopped and thought, "Well, that's one month. What about the next?"

He tore the sheet from the easel, flipping it dextrously onto the desk, and began filling the next sheet with the same, surprised young beauty now answering the front door bell. Next came the beauty as she stepped down from the Fifth Avenue bus. And then, the beauty became a bride cradling a bouquet of roses, and then a cab driver, smiling back from the driver's seat (that was bit of a stretch).

Howard spent the rest of the morning turning out sketch after sketch of the same dark beauty who kept inviting the viewer to join her in *Noir*. By lunch time he had close to a dozen ideas on paper and began composing his thoughts on convincing "Al-baire"—"Al", that is—to make the cover of *Noir* a running commentary on the beauty within and the pleasure awaiting introduction to "The Woman of *Noir*."

At lunch time Howie all but skipped down the two flights and entered the restaurant for his usual sandwich and bowl of soup. Keyed up and filled with the joy and excitement of creativity in the making, he spread the napkin and, grinning like a fool, turned to greet the owner of the hand placing before him a goblet of the King's own refreshing water.

He froze! Smiling down at him, pencil and pad in hand, was the same smiling, dark skinned beauty that he had been sketching all morning back up on the third floor. His smile disappeared, and his jaw dropped. Speechless, he stared.

The young beauty responded with matching concern. "Are you all right?"

"How long have you been working here?"

"I just started this morning," she responded, the smile edging back to where it belonged.

Howie stared, dumbfounded. "Are you a model?"

The raven beauty reacted with amusement and a slight nod of the head, saying, "Yes, but this pays a little better."

Ordering soup and sandwich was a bit chaotic, but Howie managed to get through the ritual and then down the product, all the while watching the beauty as she glided across the floor and returned with that glorious smile filled with enjoyment and the understandable curiosity.

"What's your name," he asked.

"Theresa." Again that fabulous smile.

"Well, I'm Howie, and I have a P. R. Office for *Noir Magazine* up on the third floor. Don't go anywhere or do anything foolish, because I think we have a career change for you."

Theresa ducked her head and looked at him as though she'd heard that song before, but Howie knew—exactly—what he was doing. Following "soup and sandwich," he practically skipped up to the second floor and rapped on the photographer's door.

"Come in."

In minutes Howie explained his plan. Photograph Theresa in half-a-dozen poses or more, all geared to serve as cover of the monthly magazine, *Noir*. Shooting schedule and fee to be arranged once the Editor and Owner approved the new plan. The photographer knew a good deal when he heard one, and all was agreed.

Howie bounced on up to his own office and had Al on the phone in seconds. The plan was simple. Create a cover that would attract readers to anticipate, look forward to each succeeding publication. Make *Noir* the publication every magazine stand would feature as "Cover of the Month." Make the cover do its job by leading the reader to buy—even collect—the magazine.

Al bought the idea. Theresa loved it, and the photographer began to shoot it. Within three months every newsstand in the city was featuring *Noir*, and the idea moved swiftly westward across the Hudson. Morale up in the Harlem office was swirling and swelling with every edition, and Theresa was rapidly becoming the magazine's mascot and everyone's dream girl.

Al brought her up to meet everyone and, in the process, boosted morale a hundred percent. And Theresa was having a ball. Al also made sure his wife, Sue, met the new "Queen of the Newsstand," as she was being touted, and guaranteed that Sue didn't get any mistaken impression about the new "Beauty of the Noir." Howie took the opposite approach and kept the news of the magazine's rise in popularity, with Theresa's meteoric role in the process, strictly an interoffice matter. *Noir* never saw the inside of the Andrews home, and the Andrews family knew nothing of the breadwinner's machinations.

Outside the busy world of merchandising was another matter. Families that clustered around the Philco listening to *Amos and Andy* every night also absorbed Lowell Thomas and news from Europe. As the two youngest Andrews offspring moved up the educational ladder at P.S. 8 and Howard, Jr. inched toward graduation at Tottenville High, Hitler was boldly burning the Reichstadt and marching into Poland. In response, Neville Chamberlain marched over to Germany and returned to England with "Peace in Our Time."

But the world was getting closer to the boiling point, and though Roosevelt maneuvered America into the realm of supply and demand, evidence grew that, given the course he was taking, Hitler would soon have all of Europe on his plate. England was simply an island off the coast of soon-to-be-occupied France. Even Russia was sending signals about all of Europe rapidly becoming a greater Germany. What would stop them from turning east?

The Andrews family, clustered around the Philco, mesmerized by the mellifluous Lowell Thomas, shared one common thought: America was being drawn into another World War. No one was more sensitive to such an eventuality than the one who had served in the 1914 "War to End All Wars."

Quietly, but as organized and determined as he had been with the newsboys training group in 1914, Howie resurrected the data sheet he had been given at the recruiting station long ago, the one that instructed him how to write to Washington, D.C. A new and rapidly expanding file on reenlistment was established in the West Village office of *Noir* magazine, and Howard soon learned what could be accomplished by a veteran of the 1914 "War to End All Wars."

The only problem was rank. A second lieutenant was pretty far down on the list of officer material. The fact was, West Point spewed out a classful every year. And then there were the college ROTC programs plus the new Civilian Military Training Camps springing up in places like nearby Camp Dix. Howie had to get a couple of good sized promotions if it was going to be worth going back in.

"Howie, don't you think you've done enough for your country? Wasn't the World War enough?" Ellie was close to tears as they lay in the dark going through Howie's newly disclosed plans and hopes for a return to uniform.

"This isn't a matter of how much one does," he fibbed. "It's what this country needs and what one can do to help. They're going to need Field Grade officers for an expanding army, and they need them now. Already," he added emphatically.

The best they would offer him was a one-grade promotion—a First Lieutenant. Howie was furious. He refused to accept a rank that was no better than a shavetail's with the gold plate worn off.

"Maybe it's the best thing," Ellie whispered, her gentle voice drifting across the cavernous divide between their two beds. "We need you, too," she whispered. "We need you here."

Silence took over, but Howie couldn't control the grunts and the twitches transmitted from his twin bed to hers. He fell into an uneasy sleep, assuming as he did that she was doing the same.

Breakfast was quiet. That is, until Howard, Jr. chose that moment to announce, "I've signed up for CMTC next summer." Howie froze, a mouthful of sausage preventing him—or saving him—from responding. Ellie stared at her eldest offspring, too stunned to respond.

Howie finally swallowed sufficiently to allow words to flow. "Where will you be assigned?"

"Camp Dix. It's in New Jersey."

"I know where it is," Howie snapped, a bit more irritably than intended.

Ellie almost whispered, as if fearful that her voice would trumpet up the stairs and wake the two youngest. "When do you go?"

"Oh, not until April or May. I don't have the exact date."

Howie struggled to avoid rising irritation, asking, "When do you get your commission?"

"Oh, that won't be for three years. You have to go back three years in a row before you're made Second Lieutenant." He almost laughed. "You'll still outrank me."

Howie looked at him and quietly lowered his eyes.

The meeting in Al's office was short but sweet. Howie looked at the check Al had given him as a bonus for the surge in *Noir* sales that everyone agreed was a result of Howie's cover innovation. It was generous.

"And this one's for the photographer, and this is for Theresa, both of which I'm gonna let you hand out yourself. You're the one who made it possible, so you deserve the credit."

Howie opened Theresa's envelope and peeked in at the check made out to his cover girl. He grinned, recalling Theresa's comment on how waiting on tables paid more than modeling. Not this time, he thought.

Shortly after that little exercise, Howie was skipping up the stairs to his third floor office in the West Village. He carefully laid Theresa's envelope on the sofa and put the photographer's envelope in his inside jacket pocket. Then, back out the door he went, leaving it ajar, and headed down one flight to the photographer's studio. Opening the door, he was startled to find Theresa standing topless beneath a mockup showerhead, clutching a sponge to her bare breast. Stunned but mesmerized by the sight of her bare body, at least the upper half, he simply stood and gaped. With just the trace of a smile, obviously enjoying the effect she was having on Howie, Theresa slowly lowered her sponged hand and eyed him slyly as she walked by. He had never seen anything as beautiful, even in his imagination, and couldn't help turning with her as she passed.

The photographer, witnessing the entire scene, broke the silence, explaining, "The shower water I'll etch in with a pen."

Howie turned back to find him grinning. He was obviously getting a real boot out of Howie's response while, at the same time, watching Theresa on the other side of the room reassembling her garments and slipping back into them, one by one.

Howie found himself whipping his head back and forth, watching the photographer and then Theresa, like someone at a tennis match. Finally, he gained sufficient control to call out to the now fully dressed Theresa, "Wait for me in my office. The door's open, I think. Al asked me to give you something." He couldn't help grinning himself at that. It brought a muffled guffaw from the photographer, which Howie did his best to stifle with a mouth-wide-open glare followed by assurances to Theresa that she would find it "a pleasant surprise." That brought an even louder guffaw from the photographer while Theresa slipped out into the hallway doing her best to stifle her own grin, ear-to-ear.

Howie did what he could, sheepishly bringing forth the envelope bearing the photographer's name, which he then thrust at the man, mumbling at the same time, "Here's a little something extra from Al for the work you've done and the terrific effect it's has on the magazine.

They both smirked like children till Howie finally stammered, "Gotta go. See ya later." The last thing he heard as he made his way through the door and out into the hallway was, "Take it slow and easy."

Outside in the hallway, he did his best to keep from racing up the stairwell but, nevertheless, whisked through his office door before taking a second breath and found himself standing in the middle of the office staring at Theresa. She was seated on the sofa, staring at him over Al's check stretched in front of her face between two delicate fingers just below eyes that smiled deliciously. Slowly, she lowered the check, revealing a dazzling smile. Wordlessly, she turned, slipped the check back into its envelope, deposited it in her purse and gently pushed the handbag down to the foot of the sofa.

Theresa smiled at Howie, looked over at the open door and gently rose to walk over and close it. And lock it. Howie was pivoting with her just as he had in the studio downstairs and watched her turn back to him and slowly walk over—very, very slowly. She glided to right in front of him, just below his tie, reached up and undid the knot and draped the two strands down his shoulders.

"I owe you a great deal," she said softly and slowly unbuttoned the top button on his shirt—and then the next—and the next—and the—

Time slipped by like a leaf turning a page, but it encompassed a whirlwind of pulling and tugging and slipping and clutching and scooting and bending, and . . . then, from the floor below, footsteps reverberated in the hall, and the photographer's voice echoing through the walls, "Pearl Harbor's been bombed! Pearl Harbor's been bombed." The steps reached Howie's door and gave way to fist pounding as the voice repeated the cry, "Pearl Harbor's been bombed. Pearl Harbor's been bombed."

Chapter Twenty Seven

Howie reached frantically for the trousers tossed carelessly onto the coffee table before him. Disregarding the need for—or even the lack of—under garments, he buttoned and belted what he had and then added the shirt that had been lying beside. Barefoot, tieless and coatless, he struggled with shirt buttons and stumbled toward the door, now reverberating with pounding plus the photographer's recognizable voice chanting like a broken record, "Pearl Harbor's been bombed! Pearl Harbor's been bombed!"

Turning the key that finally unlatched the door, Howie swung it open to find, no surprise to him at all, his agitated downstairs neighbor, the photographer. More shocking, however, was the lone figure standing amidst the stairs leading down to the floor below. It was his own son, Kenneth, mouth agape as he scanned his father's barefoot figure above him.

"Congress is declaring war, and Roosevelt has already sent the Navy Air Corps to go after the Japanese," the photographer went on without stopping. "Everybody's wondering what the hell the entire U. S. Pacific Fleet was doing bottled up in Pearl—"

"Where's Pearl Harbor?" Howie finally stammered.

"It's in Hawaii. The Island of Oahu. Apparently, our whole Navy—except for the Aircraft Carriers, luckily—was there, and the Japanese practically wiped them out."

At that point, Howie realized that his next-to-the-youngest son had finished climbing the stairs and passed between him and the photographer on his way to the interior of Howie's office. He spun like a ballet master and encircled Kenneth's waist with an arm as facile as a python, depositing the boy beside and a little behind the still rattling photographer. At this point, the photographer realized that the boy was there. "The boy says he's your son, Kenneth." The photographer looked at the boy and then the expression on Howie's face and then over Howie's shoulder to the familiar figure of Theresa, this time frantically grabbing bits of garment and slipping, sliding and stepping into them as she reassembled her garb, a formality he was not unfamiliar with but certainly had not expected to find in the office of his upstairs neighbor. He thought of those few, brief moments not too long ago when Howie had dropped in on the mockup of Theresa's shower scene, recalling Howie's almost ravenous stare and instructions she was to "meet him in his office upstairs." It was almost too much to allow for a straight face. But then he turned back to glance at the boy and realized from the look on young Kenneth's face just what the unspoken dialogue between father and son must be. He turned, edged past the boy and headed down the stairs, calling out as he went, "I'll see you later on, Howie. Let me know when you want to see more shots I've made. Got some great ideas."

There was a noticeable giggle as he turned the corner below, and Howie thought he also heard, "Got a couple more, too."

Acting as though on cue, Kenneth turned and raced down the stairs past the now disappearing photographer as his father called out, "Kenneth—Kenneth—Kenneth," each call becoming more and more faint—and undetermined.

Howie found himself standing at the head of the staircase, all alone, silent, wrenched like a moist rag. Then there was a soft, gentle hand between his shoulder blades, a hand that moved slowly, silently up onto his shoulder as a wry, smiling face appeared on his opposite side.

"Everyone will understand," Theresa whispered. "If not now, they will when they're your age." Then, gently, she slipped from his side and skipped down the stairs. Howie could only stare at her departing figure, stare terrified and agonized with indecision. His world spun wildly from the moment he slammed the door and finished dressing. He had transformed himself to a man driven by guilt. He would never remember the sequence of events or the details of each frantic maneuver—the demands, the reasoning, the residuals—but in the end the results were crystal clear. He had to get out. Get out of New York, break from "Noir," from Theresa, from Boudreau.

The minute he was alone and dressed he dove for the papers he had been given by the recruiting sergeant, studied them, filled a scratch pad with addresses, phone numbers and the names of those who had the slightest appearance of someone who would welcome a retread from "The War to End All Wars." Then he assembled a list of wartime experiences from the iconic Cadet Newspaper Men's Training Corps on Governor's Island through Plattsburg OCS, his Artillery training and commission as a Second Lieutenant, his Camp Meade period as a Platoon Leader—he conveniently left out that it was an all black unit except for the officers, of course—and his front line experience in France with the 92nd Div.—another case of a black unit with white officers.

Carefully, he slipped down the stairs, past the photographer's studio—pausing just a second to see if he could hear Theresa gossiping with the photographer—and then out onto the street. As fast as his legs could carry him, without having to break into a sprint, he made for the recruiting stand. His sergeant was there, just as if waiting for him.

"Well, I guess you've heard the news," was his greeting.

"What do I do?" Howie answered.

Well," drawled the sergeant, "you're what we call a "retread." I've got a special form for you to fill out, and you list the service you've had, your rank or grade, MOS, and—well, that's about it."

Howie went over his notes with the sergeant, picked up a few pre-addressed envelopes, and continued on to the Staten Island ferry. He made it the usual route to St. George, but this time he took care to sit on the starboard side of the ferry so he could look out on the Statue of Liberty as they passed. Once on the Island, he boarded the train for Great Kills, hopped off on arrival and all but flew up Nelson Avenue to the home he himself had designed for the Andrews family.

As he reached for the door handle, the door flew open, and Ellie stood ashen and speechless. She had obviously heard those same cries, though not with the same given circumstances—"Pearl Harbor's been bombed, Pearl Harbor's been bombed."

The house was quiet, and they sat alone on the sofa going over decisions that Howie had made—all alone, but decisions nevertheless. It never occurred to him that she was taking it all with not a whisper of dissent.

"I'll take these to Washington tomorrow, and I should know right away where the War Department will want me."

"Will all of us be going with you? And what about the house? Should we sell it—or try to—and will we be coming back here after the war? Oh, dear," she interjected, "how long will it last, I wonder."

"I don't want to think about that now," Howie cut her short. "Things will be entirely different when this is over, and I'll probably have a whole lot of opportunities coming out of this. Besides, there probably won't be any *Noir* magazine then. I'll have lots of things we can choose from."

There was a silence that pervaded the room for immeasurable time, broken finally by Ellie's soft whisper, "What about the children?"

"Well, Howard Junior's got his degree from Purdue, doesn't he? And didn't you say he'd been offered a job in Cleveland with some sheet metal factory? Is he interested in that?"

"Yes, I think he wants to take it, but"—she faltered—"he wants to go out there as soon as graduation is over and see what it's like."

"Well, he's old enough to make a decision like that, now, and it's a job that can't help but get bigger and better as we shift from "lend lease" to war time industry. He'll see that."

"But Kenneth and Billie are just graduating from high school."

Howie suddenly realized he had no idea what his other two boys planned to do about college. He was embarrassed to ask. "What are their plans?"

"Well, Kenneth is going to Arts Students League in New York City. He was going to tell you about it when he went in to fill out some papers this morning. He said he was going to stop by afterwards and tell you all about it." She paused. "Didn't he show up?"

Howie didn't say a word.

"One of the Tottenville classmates is also going, so they'll be sharing an apartment."

Howie was silent a moment and then asked, "Can we afford all that?"

"Yes," Ellie responded brightly. "You don't remember that your Aunt Nana left all three a thousand dollars each for college? Howard Junior's been using that for living expenses at Purdue." She obviously thrilled at how she had managed budgeting the house maintenance plus all the children's education and living. Howie was somewhat stunned at all that had been going on without his supervision.

"Billie's the only one I'm not sure about," she went on. "He wants to go into radio and plans to audition for an announcer's job once graduation is over."

"Where?"

"Well, we don't know. There's only one small station on Staten Island, and it might be hard to break into the field on Manhattan and over in New Jersey." She was obviously unsettled by those prospects.

"Well," Howie broke in excitedly, ":I was going to suggest we send both the youngest on up to Springfield. Billie can do that and stay with your folks, and I'll bet chances for a radio shot will be a lot better up there. They'll be drafting everybody now that war's declared.

There was a pause and a distinct veil of concern wafting over Ellie's countenance while Howie forced a cheerfulness into his voice. "Hell, that's a lot better than I got when my Pa had to shuffle the two of us out. How old is he, now, anyway? Fifteen, sixteen, eighteen?"

"He's sixteen. He skipped twice back in P.S. 8." Ellie dropped back into silence. The two of them sat catlike with his and her own thoughts, own concerns, own imagination of what was in store for the Andrews family. Howie held his ground. He stared at the papers in his hand and then up at Ellie. Her eyes were down. Slowly she looked up, squarely into his eyes. And she smiled.

"We'll make out just fine," she whispered.

Chapter Twenty Eight

Dinner that night was beyond even the familiar quietude of the Andrews household. The only measure of life other than the usual flicker of eyelids as the children glanced furtively at their mother coming and going from the kitchen bringing and clearing the various courses and their father looking over the serving dishes as they came and went. For the youngest three, however, the careful eye might have noticed Kenneth's sly glances in his father's direction, matched only by his father's in his. It worked almost like a ballet with no clashes. The only direct contrast had been early in the dinner when Ellie had attempted to discover what had kept Kenneth from visiting his father's office as had been planned. That subject quickly petered out, and Ellie respectfully resisted persuing it in accordance with the Andrews unwritten rules of the household. Kenneth's glances during the remainder of the evening were as furtive and lightning-like as humanly possible. Kenneth knew that there could be no open discussion of what had transpired, but he was more afraid of an accusation that he might have manufactured the story after leaving Battery Park and returning home. Howie was going through much the same mental gyrations, so his silence was virtually guaranteed just so long as the subject never came up.

Kenneth had arrived home late that afternoon and occupied himself in the back yard or closed up in his room up until dinnertime, so this had been Ellie's first opportunity to inquire, and she respected the obvious decision to remain "clammed up" without casting any aspersions on either party. Her mind churned, however, with anticipation of those late night chats across the twin bed divide. Unfortunately, the nighttime, bedtime colloquy proved just as unsettling as a foray into the office meeting would have been. What took its place was a gradual recital of Washington's decision to accept Howard Andrews in the newly organized Army Air Corps as a Captain. His first assignment would be as Squadron Commander in the equally newly organized Roswell Army Air Base in New Mexico. With almost lightning speed, Howie had booked his train ride to Roswell with promises to send for Ellie as soon as he had set up living quarters for the two of them. By then, Howie, Jr. would be settled in his new job which turned out to be in New Jersey rather than New York. Kenneth had already joined his roommate from Tottenville High at the Art Students League, and, hopefully, the house would be sold, leaving Billie free to drive his mother to Roswell and deliver both her and the car. As for Billie's future, he had surrendered to the earlier suggestion to fly to New England and settle with Ellie's family while seeking a job in radio.

All was laid out and sufficiently agreed upon in time for Howie's orders to report to Roswell and his immediate departure from New York's Penn Station. In an ironic preamble to his delivery of his mother to Roswell, Billie drove the remainder of the Andrews family minus Howie, Jr. from Staten Island, through Battery Park and over to the west side Penn Station. While he parked the car his parents and brother Kenneth shuffled listlessly in the southeast corner of Penn Station mezzanine amidst hoards scurrying by, some in clutches and others as lone streakers racing to catch a train. Howie went over last minute plans, occasionally reminding Ellie of some facet of the Great Kills house now up for sale for the first bidder their Staten Island agent could come up with.

"Don't forget to push the gold fish pond and the garden all the way back past the neighbor's house," he admonished. "Those are good selling points."

"Honey, don't worry. He's a good agent. He'll have that house sold as soon as you get a place settled for us in Roswell," Ellie assured him.

"Well, it's a good buy, and we should get a real fistful from it." He turned to Kenneth. "You got your stuff all packed?"

"Everything I have is already moved into the Manhattan apartment. Frank and I are both settled in."

Howie turned back to Ellie, his face scrunched up in puzzlement. "What was the reason you said Howard Junior couldn't be here?"

"They just got this new order—spark plugs, I think it was, for fighter planes. The whole plant got put on 24—hour duty in a rush to get them done and shipped out."

Kenneth grinned and popped in, "Yeah, they're probably heading down to Roswell Air Base. Get there about the time you will." He grinned at his father and chuckled.

Billie's voice broke through the crowd's hustle and bustle as he raced to join them. "Which track is it?," he wheezed, squeezing in between his mother and Kenneth who shoved back and then pointed over at a cluster of figures heading into one of the station's multitude of stair wells. "It's right over there."

Billie looked around at the trio for a moment and then whined, "Shouldn't we go on down to the track?"

Howie masked a grin with a well manufactured grumble as he grouched, "You trying to get rid of me?"

Ellie put her arm around Billie and pulled him to her. "Not my sweetie," she purred.

Howie grilled his son, "You ready to drive your mother all the way down to New Mexico?"

The boy responded with bravado, "Piece of cake."

Smiles and a few chuckles drew the family closer together as the wait continued and the thought of the Pater Familia, now garnished in an Army Captain's uniform, heading forth into a new life, a new world, a world they had only imagined from the scraps of conversation of the past two decades, scraps about World War One that permeated the Andrews' household and upbringing. Billie wondered what it would be like in Roswell living as an "Army brat." And for how long? Would he be able to get a job there and not go to New England? A radio announcer, maybe. That would be great stuff—worth the gamble. His mind raced back and forth, one scenario to another.

"Southwest Special! Mississippi, Louisiana, Texas, New Mexico, Arizona—track thirty-nine!" The voice roared above the Station bustle. People turned and raced—some of them—for the staircase to the cavern below.

Howie stared at Ellie, his expression a conglomeration of excitement, joy and apprehension. She pressed her cheek against his and then kissed it. The two boys watched in childish embarrassment, to witness such unusual intimacy between their parents.

Howie pulled back, stared at his betrothed a moment, glanced over at the two boys, and then, impulsively, grabbed his B-4 bag and headed for the staircase. He stopped for a moment before descending and called back to the trio, "I'll see you in a couple of weeks." Then he thought for a fraction of a second and added, "Good luck to you, Kenneth. I hope you do great and become a famous artist." Then he was swallowed up by the multitude descending to the tracks below.

Ellie moved over to the side where she could watch him reach the bottom of the staircase and the platform where the range of iron cars waited for the hoard of passengers to be swallowed up. She was able to see him head for one of the doors, stop for a moment and then step on and through the opening. It seemed to her that in that moment he straightened his shoulders and hoisted himself up just a bit.

End

www.ingramcontent.com/pod-product-compliance
Ingram Content Group UK Ltd.
Pitfield, Milton Keynes, MK11 3LW, UK
UKHW041848190726
13854UKWH00002B/767